TROUBLED SKIES

TROUBLED SKIES

DAVE JOHNSON

To all my grandchildren.

When the airship takes off, they keep me grounded.

The Rebel Runaway Series

1, Freedom Skies

2, Troubled Skies

3, Escape to the Skies (to be published in 2024)

The Stuck Series

1, Stuck in Time.

2, Stuck 1595: An Elizabethan Adventure.

3, Stuck 1824: A London Tale.

4, Stuck 1855: Lucy Travels East.

5, Stuck 1966: No Time To Groove.

6, Stuck in the Land of the Pharaohs.

7, Stuck Between Two Lives.

All "Stuck" books are stand-alone stories

CHAPTER ONE

'This is what I call shopping in style,' said Sadie.

'It certainly beats battling the waves on a three hundred and eighty-mile sea journey from the mainland,' agreed Charlotte. 'And with the wind on our tail, the Rebel will be back on Foula in no time.'

'I'm surprised this airship could get off the ground with the quantity of cogs and wheels and funny bits of metal you've got in your sack, Jake.'

'I'm glad Joshua was with us to help carry the load,' replied Jake.

'The Edinburgh street gangs had better think themselves lucky that they didn't give us any trouble because I would have made a painful dent in their heads with that bag,' chuckled Joshua.

'You're quite a celebrity in Edinburgh, Joshua. Thanks to Edward's stories, I saw all those children who think you are an African prince touching you,' said Charlotte

'Yes,' said Joshua with a laugh, 'They wanted to see if the black rubbed off my skin. I like my life much better now I am a prince than when I was a slave!'

'Anyway, it's not just my things weighing us down,' said Jake. 'We must have packages and parcels for half of the island aboard.'

'You did an excellent job, Billy, buying all the food,' commented Charlotte.

'Blimey! It's a good job you taught me to read a bit. I had a lot of shopping lists,' said Billy as he wound up the airship's clockwork motor drive.

'You've done a great job yourself, Charlotte,' said Jake. 'Isn't this the first time you've flown the Rebel without Oliver being aboard?'

'Yes, it is. I've flown it before when he's been asleep, or drunk, or usually both, but we arranged yesterday that this would be my first solo flight. Don't speak too soon, though. I've got the tricky bit to come - manoeuvring the Rebel into that crack in the cliffs!'

'I've every confidence in you, lass. I'm full of admiration!' said Sadie.

'I'm proper looking forward to wot Edward has written about us in 'is "Chronicles of the Rebel Runaways" book,' said Billy. 'That one where 'e made up a story about me cooking a bleedin' stew with a secret Chinese sleeping potion in it and sending a whole bloomin' regiment to sleep didn't 'alf make me larf.'

'I picked up a letter from him at the Post Office. A few others too. Thank heavens for the mail train. Now all the horses have died, well apart from the wild Shetland ponies on Foula, that is, it would take a long time for letters to get from London to Edinburgh on foot!' said Charlotte.

'Yours ain't the first solo flight, Charlotte. I'm hopin', the carrier pigeons I let loose in Edinburgh will 'ave found their way to the Gates of Rome.'

'By Heck! Rome? That's a long way to fly!' replied Sadie.

'No, no,' laughed Jake, 'That's more of his Cockney Rhyming Slang. I've heard that one before.'

'For the benefit of the girl from the North: Gates of Rome - home. They are flying home to Foula,' explained Billy

'Say wha tha means, can't tha?' Sadie replied, in a much broader Lancashire accent than usual.

'By Jove, we can send messages with our feathered friends in the future,' said Billy in the poshest voice he could manage.

'Shush now, everyone. I need to concentrate. Foula is ahead, and as usual, it's very windy; we don't want the story to end before it starts with us being dashed on the cliffs!"

In a sumptuous office in Number Ten Downing Street, the former home of the ousted prime minister and now the residence of Field Marshal Bellings, the leader of the new military government, a tetchy meeting was taking place between Bellings and the richest and most powerful industrialist in the country, Leonard Fotheringay.

'Olethros! What kind of name is that?' demanded Bellings.

'It's the Greek God of Chaos.'

'Chaos! We are supposed to be on the side of law and

order, for goodness' sake!

'I mean in the sense that we will cause chaos among the protesters. When faced with its power, they will scatter.'

'I can tell you now. There is no way the rank and file soldiers who will be operating this new machine of yours will get their tongues around Olethros.'

'Good point,' agreed Fotheringay, 'How about Cerberus?'

'It's easier to say, but who or what was Cerberus?'

'In Greek legends, he was a monstrous dog with three heads and a serpent for a tail who guarded the gates to the Underworld. My machine has three cannons mounted on the front that will unleash havoc on an unruly crowd.'

'Alright, Cerberus, it is then. When will it be ready? My spies are giving me reports that the Trades Union movement is planning unrest.'

'It's near completion now. I just need to get our blacksmith to strengthen the waggon's axles because it's a heavy beast.'

'Beast! Now that's a name I like. We'll call it "The Beast". Keep me posted.'

As Fotheringay left Bellings' office, he thought to himself, 'It's hard to believe that such an unsophisticated man is running our country. Still, I have to appease him as his patronage will make me a wealthy man. Or should I say, an even more wealthy man!'

Bellings hadn't even waited for Fotheringay to leave his office before he started to mutter to himself.

'Olethros? Cerberus? I ask you. Just who is he trying to impress with all his fancy Greek nonsense? I got my education the hard way, on the battlefield. Admittedly, I went to Oxford, but you never caught me with my nose in a book. Especially a Greek one! However, our relationship has to be fostered if I am going to prosper financially. A man has debts and expenses, after all. It's all very well being in charge of the country, but I'll be damned if I can direct any money from the treasury my way! Still, the shipping venture he's planning sounds like an ideal way of injecting a great deal of cash into my account, so I will just have to put up with him!'

Everyone agreed that Charlotte was the best narrator, so she read Edward's new story to everyone sitting around the kitchen table at the Laird of Foula's house. They were enthralled, not just because the plot featured themselves but also because it was a story that Edward had invented. He had used up all their real-life adventures in a series of booklets that had made the Rebel Runaways much-loved household names throughout Britain. Even the staff of the Fotheringay household were avid readers of the stories that included their master's errant daughter, although they took care to keep copies well hidden.

'Cor blimey, we'll 'ave to go out and 'ave a few cheeky adventures for ourselves!' laughed Billy. 'My life is a bit boring compared with the Billy in the story!'

'I had every faith in Edward being able to write a good tale,' said the Laird, Alexander, 'He even makes my brother come out smelling of roses.' Oliver smiled. It was true; Edward tended to gloss over the fact that he often drank too much alcohol!

'What's in Edward's letter?' asked Jake. Charlotte was silent as she looked through it. When she spoke, her voice had a tremor.

'It concerns my father. I had put him out of my mind lately. As well as making up stories, Edward has been investigating more serious matters. He has been to a relatively new institution called Companies House which keeps a record of all British businesses. Edward has discovered that my father and uncle have a company in partnership with a shipping agent named Greville.'

'That's interesting,' said Jake, 'In case you don't know, Sadie, Charlotte's uncle, Robert Fotheringay, was a slave owner, and it was from him that Joshua escaped when he overheard plans for a slaving expedition.'

'And that's about as far as Edward can get with his research. Any other details will be in the offices of the shipping agent,' continued Charlotte.'

'Hmm!' commented Oliver, pulling off his boot and scratching his foot, 'Is anyone else getting itchy feet?'

By way of response, everyone in the room, except Alexander and Cissie, his housekeeper, took their boots off, wiggled their toes and shouted:

'Yes! Yes! Yes!'

'So what exactly are we doing out here on the moor?' asked Sadie. She had just watched Joshua hammer three stakes into the peat after first chasing away some Great Skuas, the giant seabirds which had previously had the place to themselves. Atop of each post was fixed a rectangle of wood, in the middle of which was painted a circle. 'They look a bit like targets,' she said.

'Well. That's because it's exactly what they are,' replied Jake, delving into the sack at his feet. 'This is why I didn't want us to leave for London until we were ready. Let me introduce you to the Glove and the Gauntlet, and I am going to test my own one, which I have called The Dart.' Jake produced an object that resembled a gloved hand pointing with one finger, made of copper, lace and leather. 'You did say you were both right-handed, didn't you?' Joshua and Sadie nodded. 'If you look inside, you will see there is a fitting to grab hold of, and next to where your thumb will stick out is a button. It's a trigger. I'll demonstrate.' Jake slipped the Glove over his right hand, then flipped a lever mounted on the back, 'This is important; it's a safety catch. Now I'll aim and press the trigger.' There was a quiet clicking noise as the clockwork mechanism activated the springs, and then a dart shot out heading for the target.

'Missed,' said Jake, 'But never mind. That's why we are here; to get some practice. The Glove, Sadie, is for you.' Jake flipped the safety catch on and handed it to Sadie. 'It's got six darts fitted, so always put the safety catch on before you take it off, or else you might end up skewering your foot.'

'It's heavier than it looks,' complained Sadie.

'That's because there are a lot of moving parts hidden inside,' said Jake, 'I was worried about that; look at the wrist area, see how there is a dimple?' Jake reached into his sack and pulled out a cane topped with a round silver knob,' Now see this, it's extendible. A quick twist locks it in place, and the silver ball on top slots into the dimple on the wrist.'

'It'll only be reet for short periods,' said Sadie, frowning.

'But not if you are using these,' replied Jake, pulling a bandoleer out of his sack: a narrow strip of canvas into which were inserted dozens of darts. 'As I said, it's a six-shooter, but if you slip one of these into the slot on the side, it will keep reloading.'

'Do I have one like that?' asked Joshua.

'The Gauntlet is similar, said Jake, reaching into the sack once more. 'Only just like your muscles, this one is massive. It fits over the whole of the arm. It contains springs ten times more powerful than the Glove and fires more of a harpoon than a dart, to which a rope can be attached. It may be useful, for example, if we want to tether the Rebel to something. In that instance, you'll fit a spear with barbs so it won't pull out, but this one doesn't, so that you can reuse it. We'll spend the rest of the afternoon practising. I'll fit my dart hand.' Jake fitted the new contraption onto his left wrist. He had come a long way since the days when all he had there was a rudimentary hook.

'Hand in the glove,' said Sadie, repeating Jake's instructions, 'Rest on the cane, safety catch off and… Hell's Bells! That trigger is sensitive!' She watched her dart streak across the moor and strike a bird sitting on the target. With a squawk and a puff of feathers, it toppled over, stone dead.

'Oh dear,' said Jake. 'It looks like you have skewered a Skua!

CHAPTER TWO

'More tea?'

'I don't mind if I do, Mary,' replied Oliver. 'Thank you.'

Oliver, Billy and Charlotte had spent the day delivering gifts of candles to the inhabitants of Foula. Jake's friend Maggie had made them in London, and now that a return to the capital was imminent, Oliver thought he might as well dole out his remaining stocks as he would soon be able to replenish his supply. The round of visits allowed him to chat with everyone, find out any news, and help ensure that the Islanders fully accepted the Rebel Runaways. The locals all knew the authorities shouldn't get wind that they were resting up in the Shetland Islands after their adventures down South. Mary lived in a little cottage near the jetty; hers was the last stop.

'And how are your two boys, Mary?' Oliver asked.

'It's hard tae believe they're twins," she replied, "They dinnae look alike, and they certainly dinnae behave the same. They're like chalk and cheese. Jamie is daein' just fine. He's got his ain boat the noo. He snags lobsters and sells them tae the posh restaurants on the mainland. He's guid company. I'm expectin' him back later the day; he wis awa' early this mornin' tae sell at Edinburgh's fish market.'

'And Finlay?' asked Oliver, 'I heard he'd moved to the mainland.'

'Ach, he's in Embra. Jamie sees him noo an' again, usually when Finlay wants tae borrow some money. Nae that he ever gies it back. Ah'm worried aboot Finlay; he's gotten himsel' mixed up wi' a bad crewd an' disnae want tae pit in a day's graft tae earn an honest bob.' Just then, the door burst open to reveal a muscular, suntanned man with windswept hair.

'Jamie!' cried his mother, delighted to see him, 'I wisnae expectin' ye sae sune. Did ye no' share a few drams wi' yer pals after ye docked?'

'No, Ma, Ah came straight here tae tell ye that Fin is oan the island. He came tae see me at the market tae ask fur a ride. He's wi'a couple 'o tough-lookin' Edinburgh boys. Weel, they're nae lookin' sae tough noo 'cause they're baith seasick and restin' up at the dock a wee while.'

'It's funny he should bring folk frae Embra wi' him tae see his Ma,' said Mary.

'That's jist it, Ma. I only heard snatches o' conversation, but I dinnae think seein' ye is the reason he has come.'

'Why else would he come tae Foula?'

'Dinnae ken, Ma. He kept tellin' the Edinburgh boys

that he was gonnae mak' them rich. He said it was a secret an' he wad show them. I think they are nane the wiser either.'

Oliver rose and shook Jamie's hand.

'I think we had better get going. Nice to see you, Jamie.'

'And thanks for the tea and the shortbread, Mary,' added Billy, 'It was proper tasty. You'll 'ave to show me 'ow to make it. I've 'ad a go, but mine's not a patch on yours!' For a brief moment, Mary smiled in delight before her brow creased with worry again about her errant son.

Outside, Oliver turned to Charlotte.

'Are you thinking what I'm thinking?' Charlotte nodded. 'There is only one thing that could conceivably be thought of as valuable on this island, and that is, as far as we know, the last remaining herd of ponies in Great Britain. Maybe the last in the world.'

'Would he be the sort to sell that secret, perhaps to the army?' asked Charlotte.

'I'm afraid so. I know the boy. He's not trustworthy. He's always had a chip on his shoulder, perhaps because his brother, Jamie, is bigger and stronger. I think his father, when he was alive, was a bit hard on him,' replied Oliver, 'That didn't help.'

'Oh, that's a shame and a worry, too,' said Charlotte. 'The ponies would be of no use to the cavalry, but they could be pack animals. Instead of running wild and free in the Shetlands, they might end their days pulling heavy cannons on the battlefield.'

'Can we shoo the ponies away so the Edinburgh boys never see 'em?' asked Billy.

'I think that's the best we can do,' replied Oliver, 'And we have to make sure those two ruffians get back home safely. As much as I would like to dump them in the ocean, we can't risk others coming to look for them if they disappear. Billy, run back and tell the others what's happening. We'll need their help. Charlotte and I will get the Rebel.'

'Ach! What hae you bought us to this God-forsaken hell hole for ye skinny wee runt!' groaned Pockets.

'Ye'll be thankin' me soon,' replied Finlay, 'Ah tell ye, play yer cards right, an' we'll aw be rich.'

Pockets had earned his nickname because he always wore a coat with voluminous pockets, and it was from one of these that he now produced a bottle of whisky and took a swig before passing it on to his companion, Fuse. This man had gained his nickname by being short and having a very quick temper. Once his fuse was lit, extreme violence was inevitable.

'Play yer cards right,' growled Fuse. 'That's a bit rich coming fae you, seein' how ye owe me twenty quid fra playin' poker!'

'And dinnae forget whit ye owe me,' said Pockets, taking back the whisky bottle before Finlay could have any. 'So, will ye tell us noo why we're here?'

'No yet; I dinnae want tae spoil the surprise. Are ye ready tae stert walkin'?'

'My brain is ready, but my legs aren't so sure, and as for my stomach, it disnae ken whit it wants to do! Alright, lead on Thin; it had better be worth it.'

Finlay didn't care for his nickname, Thin. He had tried to get the others in the gang to call him Fin, but they wouldn't because Thin was such an apposite name, there wasn't an ounce of extra flesh on him, nor muscle either.

Finlay achieved results by cunning, rather than brute strength. Unfortunately, Fin never seemed to benefit from his sly schemes, perhaps because he wasn't as intelligent as he thought he was.

'Aye, this time I'll be quids in. Just ye wait and see, Jamie; I'll show ye,' he thought.

A mile away, on the moor, Oliver descended the rope ladder to talk to the rest of the crew assembled on the ground, whilst Charlotte kept the airship hovering above.

'Fin and his companions are bound to walk this way, and it's unlikely that the ponies would ever come down this far. Two of you should stay here and keep an eye on the three men, but stay out of sight. There are enough rocks to hide behind,' instructed Oliver.

'I'll stay,' said Jake.

'And me,' added Sadie.

'The rest of you come up inside the Rebel, and we will go and look for the ponies,' continued Oliver, 'Good, I see you've brought some brightly-coloured scarves from the costume trunk. Jake and Sadie, you can wave them to signal that our visitors are near. The others can use them to frighten the horses away from these troublemakers.'

And so began a bizarre game of cat and mouse in which the three visitors from Edinburgh were completely unaware they were participating. Everyone except Charlotte and Billy was on the ground, and Charlotte kept the airship well away from Fin and his friends. Mostly she flew as low as she dared, which helped scare the ponies away. Occasionally she rose rapidly to hide above the clouds. Meanwhile, Jake and Sadie found it easy to follow the three unwelcome visitors by hiding behind the rocky outcrops, while staying near enough to overhear their conversations.

'Ouch!' Fuse had stubbed his toe. 'I'm sick o' this

noo.' Pockets laughed at his friend's misfortune. Finlay made the mistake of joining in with the laughter, which garnered a dark look from Fuse. Finlay quickly clamped his mouth shut.

'I cannae unnerstaun it," grumbled Finlay. "We should hae seen them by noo.'

'Seen whit?' demanded Fuse.

'I wantit it tae be a surprise.'

'I'll tell ye whit's a suprise. It's the fact that I've pit up wi' yer nonsense for sae lang.'

'I tell ye, we can aw be rich,' whined Finlay.

'Ouch!' Fuse had stubbed his toe again. 'Firstly, ye are no' in a position tae tell me onythin', ye wee pile o' dug's muck, and secondly, who said onythin' aboot ye becomin' rich?' A seabird dived at the group, scattering them as they flapped their arms to try and frighten it away. Having grown up on the island, Finlay was used to attacks like these and knew they must be near the bird's nest.

'It's just a skua,' he said with a nervous laugh. This was another mistake. Fuse was not inclined to be cheerful. His face darkened.

'That's it! Ah've haed enough o' yer get-rich trickery. Gie's whit ye owe me noo.'

'But, Ah cannae," stammered Finlay.

'Canna or winnae?" threatened Fuse.

'Ah huvnae goat it.'

'Ah thoat we were comin' tae fynd some treasure ye hid here.'

'Naw, naw. Ah want tae shaw ye a secret that'll mak oor fortunes. A've goat this notion.'

'Y're tryin' tae bribe me wi' an idea? I'll say it again. Gie's whit ye owe me.' Fuse advanced on Finlay, who retreated until his back was pressed against a large rock.

'Ah cannae, but when we are rich, I...' Fuse interrupted him:

'I'll tell ye whit, wi' the siller ye owe, I'm gonna cut ma losses. I'll wipe the slate clean.'

'Oh! Thanks, Fuse, I...' Finlay was interrupted by a searing pain as Fuse's knife slipped between his ribs, and he crumpled to the floor.

'Waste o' space!" commented Pockets, 'Although ye might hae waited until he showed us the way back tae civilisation!'

'Aye. He got ma dander up. Let's try this way. I think we came frae there, although I reckon he was leadin' us aroond in circles.'

The two men turned and walked away. Meanwhile, Sadie and Jake crept out from behind the rock to investigate. They had heard the conversation but couldn't figure out what had happened. It was worse than they could have imagined. Finlay was curled up on the ground with blood oozing from his chest.

'Oh no! What shall we do, Jake?' asked Sadie.

'Press something against his wound to try and stop the bleeding. I'll run back and attract the attention of the others. They can't see us now as they are following a track that bends around the rocks.' Sadie found a handkerchief in Finlay's pocket, rolled it into a ball and pressed it against his chest. She certainly was not going to ruin her scarf by getting it covered in blood! Meanwhile, Jake ran towards where he had last seen the others, furiously waving his scarf. It was obvious that he wanted attention because he was out in the open. When Joshua and Oliver reached him and heard what had happened, they rushed over to join Sadie.

'It doesn't look good,' said Oliver. 'I saw many wounds on the battlefield when I was a soldier and I don't rate his chances of survival very highly, but we can't leave him here to die. I know his mother.'

'There's a second problem,' said Jake, 'If the intention is to make sure the two villains get back to Edinburgh, then I noticed that they've taken the wrong path. Should Sadie and I appear to encounter them by chance and guide them back to the jetty?'

'That's a good idea. It goes against the grain to let them get away with it, but we don't want police from the mainland here. The villains probably haven't even thought about how they will get back to Edinburgh. Finlay's brother, Jamie, won't be taking them. If he did, they would end up in a watery grave. Tell any fisherman willing to take them that I will cover the cost of a journey. Joshua, lift Finlay up, and we'll get out in the open and try to attract Charlotte's attention. She will get him back home quicker than we can walk.'

'If ye tell me one mair time that we're scunnert oot in circles, ye'll gang the same wey as Thin and feel the shairp end o' ma knife,' growled Fuse.

'And how dae ye think that'll gie ye an oot frae this cursed island?' retorted Pockets.

'It'll mak me feel better. I shouldnae hae come. It wis yer idea tae folla Thin's nonsense.'

'It wasnae!'

'Good afternoon.' The two men spun round in surprise, to be greeted by the sight of Jake and Sadie. 'Are you out for a little stroll like us, enjoying the views?' asked Jake.

'Whit wey tae the port?' was Fuse's terse response.

'We're going that way ourselves,' replied Jake, 'We can show you the way.'

For the next fifteen minutes, they followed the path towards the sea.

'How long noo?' whined Fuse. He kept glancing at Jake's metal hand. The sight of it appeared to bother him.

'Another fifteen minutes,' Jake replied.

'Ach. Weel, ah think the wee lassie here can show us the rest o' the way. Ye neednae stick aroond,' said Fuse.

'Oh! But we are walking together,' replied Jake. Fuse turned to face Jake and opened the front of his coat to reveal the knife stuck in his belt.

'Tell me, laddie, which pairt o' whit ah said did ye no' unnerstaun?'

'Oh, yes, I see, Quite,' replied Jake, acting more flustered than he actually felt.

'It's quite alright,' said Sadie demurely, 'I can see these good gentlemen to the jetty. You don't need to worry about me.'

'Goodbye, then,' said Jake, 'I'll go another way; I'll follow the path around that big rock.'

CHAPTER THREE

Jake wasn't at all worried about Sadie. One thing that her former life as a prostitute had taught her was how to manipulate men. She also had her new weapon, the Glove, and Jake sensed she wouldn't hesitate to use it.

Two paths led to the jetty from a huge rock standing proud on the moor. Sadie took the one on the right, while Jake took the shorter, left hand route. Sadie guessed that he wanted to get to the harbour before she did so he could find someone willing to give the two men a passage to Edinburgh.

'So, ye were walkin' wi' that young lad, but are ye walkin' oot wi' him, if ye ken whit I mean?' asked Fuse in a tone that he intended to sound light-hearted but which still came across as aggressive.

'Oh, no! Definitely not,' replied Sadie.

'Aye, well, he fair gied me the willies wi' that metal hand o' his,' said Pockets, taking a whisky bottle from his coat and gulping a slug before passing it on to Fuse.

'Whit ye need, lassie, is a real man,' said Fuse, tapping his chest to indicate that he was a prime example. 'Try this!' He passed her the whisky bottle. She lifted it to her lips.

'Oh my!' she coughed. The two men didn't notice that her thumb was over the mouth of the bottle, so no drop passed her lips. She pretended to take another swig, 'Lawks-a-mussy! I could get used to this!'

'That's ma girl,' said Fuse admiringly. The bottle passed its way around the threesome on the journey back to the harbour until finally it was empty, and Pockets tossed it aside, where it smashed upon a rock. Sadie inwardly winced at this desecration of the landscape, but she maintained a friendly demeanour. 'Dinnae worry; I've got mair whisky in ma poke,' said Pockets with a grin.

'By yer accent, ye're no' fae these pairts, are ye?' asked Fuse.

'No, I'm from Manchester, but I've spent a long time living in London.'

'Sassenach towns full of heathens. Tell me, hae ye ever been tae Edinburgh?'

'No,' lied Sadie, 'But I'd love to see it.' For the rest of the walk to the jetty, the two men extolled the virtues of the city of their birth. They did not mention art galleries and museums, the Castle and other historical monuments, nor the shops and restaurants. Instead, they gave a detailed account of all the pubs they frequented and the status they had earned by being "real men" in a hard city.

At last, they arrived at the harbour. Sadie, unlike her companions, wasn't in the slightest bit intoxicated and had her wits about her. As she expected, Jake had already arrived and was leaning against a wall, pointing at one of the fishing boats. She gave him a surreptitious wave, and he nodded and left to wait for her out of sight.

'I'll have a word with a fisherman for you,' said Sadie, and strolled over to talk to the man swilling down the deck of the boat that Jake had pointed to.

'I've sorted it all out,' she said brightly when she returned. 'I'll say goodbye, then.'

'Nay, lassie,' replied Fuse, 'It wad be a shame tae pairt company noo.' He took a firm grip of her arm, 'Ye said ye wanted tae see Embra. We'll gie ye a good time,' and he winked at Pockets.

Jake's heart sank as he spied what was happening. Intervening would not be sensible, as violence would certainly ensue, and the Rebel Runaways' plans to coax the two men back to Edinburgh would be ruined. He still had no concerns in the short term about Sadie's well-being, but he knew that the airship would have to return to Edinburgh. Sadie may not need help, but she would certainly need a lift back to the island. By now Oliver would be at Finlay's mother's house, but Jake was unsure where that was. On the other hand, finding Charlotte should be easy. He just needed to look up to the sky.

Mary knelt on the floor, cradling Finlay's head in her lap. Blood stained the stone floor. Jamie had torn Finlay's shirt into strips to make a bandage and tied it tightly around his brother's chest, but the blood continued to seep through it. Finlay kept drifting in and out of consciousness. Oliver, looking on, knew that the prognosis was not good.

'Oh, my poor wee boy,' sighed Mary. Finlay opened

his eyes for a moment and looked up at his mother.

'Ah'm sorry, Ma,' he whispered, 'Ah jist wanted tae show ye and Jamie that Ah was worth somethin'. Ah wanted tae mak ye proud o' me..'

'Aye be at peace noo, Finlay, ma bonnie bairn. Yer Mammy loves ye very much.'

There was silence in the room until Finlay gave one last rasping breath. Then silence again.

'He's gone,' said Mary quietly, and she began to weep.

Fuse threw the last empty bottle of whisky into the water just before the boat docked on the mainland at the Port of Leith.

'A cannae get any closer tae the city centre,' said Tom, the fisherman.

'Aye, this'll dae,' replied Pockets, 'They know us here,' and he clambered onto dry land.

'Are ye gonnae be awricht?' whispered Tom to Sadie before Fuse had roused himself, They've haed a lot o' whisky!'

'Don't worry. I can handle myself. Oliver will pay you handsomely for the journey.'

'What's that?' slurred Fuse, gripping her by the arm, 'Who are ye callin' handsome?'

'Why you, of course,' she replied. Staying on the boat was not an option.

'Come on youse,' called Pockets, 'We've got a house call tae make.' They walked a short distance before stopping outside a small stone warehouse. "Jackson and Sons. Exporters of the Finest Whisky" was displayed above the door, and Pockets part stumbled, part swaggered inside. Sadie, who had successfully avoided drinking anything, was amazed by the two men's capacity for alcohol, but at last, it was beginning to show. After a few minutes, Pockets emerged from the warehouse clutching two bottles. One disappeared inside his oversized coat, and he drew the cork from the other and took a deep draft before passing it on to Fuse.

'As ah said,' laughed Pockets, 'They ken us here. They widnae dare refuse me this wee present tae keep us sweet!'

'That's only one person who has seen one of them on Scottish soil. It will be better if others who know them have seen both. Then I'll try and slip away,' thought Sadie. 'Where are we going?' she asked.

'We've goat a place under the arches o' the Sooth Bridge. Mibbe no the area it aince wis, but folk let us be. It suits us. The polis willnae come lookin' there!'

Thirty minutes later, Fuse stopped outside a public house. 'We're nae far awa', but ah've goat a richt thirst. Ah reckon it's aw that sea air. A quick swally in The Thistle shuid rinse awa' the sailt.' He took hold of Sadie's arm and led her into the tiny, dark pub. It was quite crowded, but everyone seemed to ignore her, so she sat in an empty nook at the back and waited for her two 'escorts'. No one ignored Fuse and Pockets, though. It was obviously a regular haunt of theirs.

'Fuse! Lang may yer lum reek!'

'You're lookin' scunnered there, Pockets.'

'Ach, a weel, it's been a lang day.'

Sadie had no choice other than to drink her beer, but as it was the first alcohol she had consumed that day, it wasn't a problem and in any case she was feeling quite thirsty. Fuse and Pockets had hemmed Sadie in, so she couldn't escape yet, but at least she knew that when the moment came, she would have succeeded in her task. The two men were safely back in their home city.

'Aye, ma bonnie wee lassie. Time tae go,' said Fuse, pulling Sadie roughly to her feet. She soon found herself in the unenviable position of being escorted through Edinburgh's slums by the two villains. Street urchins scattered as they approached; they knew better than to try and beg them for money. Drunks, lolling in doorways, hailed them.

'All in all, this reminds me of The Rookery in London and my time working at Madam Boo-Boo's,' thought Sadie. Many of the women on the streets were certainly prostitutes; they looked like they had fallen on hard times and been pickled in gin.

'Here we are, the Sooth Bridge Vaults,' announced Pockets producing a key from his coat. 'There's nineteen o' these walled-in arches, but we've goat one o' the better yins cause oors is split intae twa floors.' It was dark inside. The squalid living space wasn't improved much when Pockets lit a few lamps.

'First, a wee dram,' Pockets said as he locked the entrance door from the inside. Sadie wasn't sure how big a dram was, but Pockets took a huge swig of whisky. As if in competition, Fuse seized the bottle and did likewise. Being outside after sitting in the pub had made them unsteady on their feet. Fresh air often did that to a drinker, Sadie knew, although you could hardly call the atmosphere fresh in here. It smelled putrid. The two men passed the bottle around again, and Sadie pretended to drink. For the first time, she felt uneasy. She noticed a dirty mattress on the floor in the corner.

'So, ye'll be gaun up the stairs then, mon,' said Fuse, gesturing to a ladder, 'While I...' He winked at Pockets, who was slumped on a stool.

'I dinnae see why ah should go second,' said Pockets angrily. 'A've keepit ye in drink a' day,'

'Yer havnae paid fur any o' it, as ye weel ken. Ye, pal, are second.' Sadie was getting increasingly annoyed at being discussed as though she wasn't there. She reached inside her bag and located the Glove.

'Wha says ah'm gaun second?' shouted Pockets.

'Ah say,' replied Fuse angrily, and he brandished his knife at Pockets. Then, it all happened too quickly for Sadie to see properly what had happened. It appeared that Fuse had jabbed with his knife at the same time as Pockets had tried to get up from his stool. Pockets stumbled, and as time appeared to stand still, Sadie saw that he now had a knife lodged in his windpipe. He clawed the air for a moment, then collapsed.

'Ach! Ye fool!' spat Fuse. 'Whit did ye dae that fur? I wis only gonna gie ye a wee scratch as a warnin.' Sadie gave a gasp of horror. Fuse turned to her, 'Listen, dinnae ye breathe a word o' this, ye unnerstaun?'

'But, but..' Sadie was silenced by a backhand swipe from Fuse that made her stagger back.

'Da'e ye hear me? Nae a word! Noo we've goat business tae dae.'

'But, don't you think...?' Fuse raised his arm to slap Sadie again, but this time, he didn't land a blow on her face; instead, he clutched at his chest with both hands at the spot where a dart from Sadie's Glove had pierced his heart.

Sadie then set to work. She found another knife tucked into Pockets' belt, dipped it in the pool of his blood and closed his fingers around it. She wrapped the dart sticking out of Fuse's chest with the tail of his shirt to gain a better grip, and placing her foot on his chest, she tugged the dart until it came free, then wiped it clean on the shirt and put it in her bag. She gathered several empty whisky bottles that were strewn about the room and placed them near the half-empty bottle that lay close to Fuse. She surveyed the scene for a moment. Eventually, someone would discover the men and it would look like they had killed each other in a drunken argument, which was half true. She had one more thing to do: the rather unpleasant task of delving into Pockets' coat until she found the door key amongst several other dubious items. Finally, she slipped out of the door, leaving it ajar to increase the chances of the street urchins finding the bodies before Fuse and Pockets turned into skeletons.

Sadie set off walking to a more salubrious part of town; street urchins clamoured around her and drunks and beggars called after her, but she passed through them as easily as a knife cuts butter. She felt no remorse or anxiety. She was untouchable.

'Hello,' said Sadie cheerily as she entered Bruce Robertson's shop. 'I'm Sadie; I have met you once before with Oliver. To be honest, when I'm in Edinburgh, I usually spend my time shopping for clothes, but I was wondering if you had seen Jake today?'

'Why no. It's not been long since he bought a supply of cogs and springs from me. Has he used them up already?'

'No, it's just that I had to come into Edinburgh unexpectedly, and I imagine he is looking for me. This is the one place I know he always comes when he's in town.'

'You are welcome to sit and wait. Would you like a cup of tea?'

'Tell me,' said Sadie later as they drank their beverages,

'How is day-to-day life in the city these days?'

'It's not getting any easier, but it could be worse. I hear the gangs in London have formed an alliance which must make them a considerable threat. Ours spend their time fighting each other, so it takes off a wee bit of pressure, although you don't know who will come through the door demanding money for so-called protection from one day to the next. It's a blessing to have a boy like young Jake as a customer. Someone who is trying to create new things rather than trying to get money for nothing!'

'Speak of the devil,' said Sadie as Jake walked into the shop, 'Here he is!'

'Hello, Sadie, I was hoping I would find you here. I traced you to a pub called The Thistle, but no one knew where you went after that. Is everything alright? Are you alright?'

'I'm fine. It's all taken care of.'

'I don't want to pry into your business,' said Bruce, 'I'll make you a cup of tea.'

'It was all we could do to stop Jamie sailing to Edinburgh to seek revenge,' said Jake, once Bruce had left the room, 'Oliver told him his place was with his mother, but I'm sure once his brother is buried, he will be over.'

'Tell him there is no need. As I said, I have dealt with it. They've give up taking sugar.'

'Pardon,' said Jake, 'What on earth does that mean?'

'Ah, it's an expression we use in Lancashire. They won't be taking sugar in their tea anymore because they are dead!'

'What's in that box you are carrying?' asked Thomas, returning with a fresh pot of tea.

'It's one of Billy's carrier pigeons,' replied Jake. 'I'm going to write a message right now to attach to the bird's leg, and she will be home before we are, taking the good news back to Foula. All is well. The Rebel Runaways have successfully concluded this chapter.'

CHAPTER FOUR

'It's taken us a little longer to leave Foula than we planned with having to attend poor Finlay's funeral, but here we are now. The Thames is below us, although it's too dark and foggy to see it,' said Oliver.

'Do you remember the last time we were in London and staying at what we thought was your friend's house?' laughed Jake.

'And blimey, we only went and ended up at the wrong bleedin' gaff!' added Billy, joining in with the laughter.

'If you hadn't drunk so much, Oliver, you could have told us the correct house number!' admonished Charlotte.

'Alright, alright,' replied Oliver, 'No need to remind

me. This time Edward has booked rooms for us at the Central Hotel again.'

'Where lovely young Tom works?' asked Charlotte.

'That's right. Edward has already slipped the manager a little sweetener so he doesn't tell the authorities about us.'

'What have you been up to, Jake?' asked Charlotte, 'You've been hard at work most of the time on this long flight back to London.'

'I'll show you,' replied Jake. 'I just needed to add a few finishing touches to my new hand. I call it the Tool Kit. It's got a clockwork motor drive. There are five buttons on the back, and when I press them, each digit turns into a different tool. See, my thumb becomes an adjustable wrench, my first finger is a screwdriver, the next has a saw, and so on. Now that I've finished it, I can continue working on my next invention, the Spider.'

'Ah'm not frit of many things, but I don't like spiders,' complained Sadie.

'Oh! You'll like this one.' Jake reached inside a sack and pulled out a segmented copper ball resembling a peeled tangerine. He flung it up in the air, and on contact with the airship's deck, eight legs shot out, and it started to spin furiously.

'Oh, that's cute,' laughed Charlotte, 'It's like a child's toy!' Jake picked it up, the legs retracted, and once again, it was a ball.

'It will have another function. A saw blade will emerge, and the Spider will be able to cut a hole in wood up to three inches thick,' said Jake.

'Well done, Jake, said Oliver. 'Now, I need everyone to be on guard duty. In a few moments, I will drop below the clouds, and hopefully, we will be pretty close to Blackwall, where we can hide the Rebel in our secret tunnel.

I need lookouts all around the gondola. Since our last little adventure, I am sure the military government will have tasked the Air-Fleet with tracking us down, so scan the skies for other airships or balloons. Hopefully, it's so early in the morning that no one will notice us.'

Jake had to resist the urge to pop into the British Museum. Now that he was a well-dressed man about town, he could walk in through the front door rather than having to climb in through an upstairs window, as in his former life, but just now he had something more important to do. With him, as he walked down Chancery Lane, were Sadie and Charlotte. His own clothes were rather sedate. He would normally wear a top hat decorated with cogs, but today he sported a plain black one. He had even left his beloved goggles behind. Jake wanted to blend in, so most importantly, bespoke black leather gloves concealed the metal hand he called his Tool Kit.

Sadie and Charlotte, however, were wearing their Rebel Runaway finest! Both had corsets worn outside their dresses and an abundance of petticoats which showed just enough leg to upset Victorian morality. These clearly were two ladies who neither wanted nor expected to be ignored.

'We had better space ourselves out now,' said Jake. He hung back to allow the girls to walk in front of him, and when they arrived at Haddon House, Charlotte led the way. With every sway of her hips and flounce of her petticoats, Charlotte found her nerves evaporating. She knew where the stairs were from the description of the building that Edward had given them, so she barely looked at the porter sitting behind a desk near the door.

'Greville and Wynne,' she announced and briskly

walked up to the second floor where the offices were situated. The porter had hardly had time to recover his composure, never having encountered anybody dressed like Charlotte before, when the routine was repeated, this time when Sadie entered the building.

'Greville and Wynne,' said Sadie, feeling quite anxious. This was her first excursion out in the field.

'Excuse me, Miss,' said the porter, rising from his chair. However, at that moment, Jake appeared.

'I say,' he said, knocking his metal hand on the desk to attract the porter's attention. 'Excuse me, Sir, I said "Excuse me".' He had succeeded in causing a distraction because, by now, Sadie had disappeared from sight. 'Tell me, please, is this the right building for the offices of Greville and Wynne?'

'I don't believe it!' said the porter. 'Nobody all day and then three people in the space of a few minutes. You may as well join the party. Second Floor. Mr Greville won't see you without an appointment, you know.'

'That's alright,' thought Jake as he bounded up the stairs, 'I don't particularly want him to see me.' Jake waited until he could hear Charlotte and Sadie in action before quietly slipping into the office. One thing Charlotte and Sadie were not doing was being quiet!

'You tell him to get his lying, cheating body out here,' screeched Charlotte at one of the four unfortunate young men sitting astonished at their desks in the large anteroom.

'It's me that wants to see him!' shouted Sadie, and then turning her attention to Charlotte, she yelled, 'And you can clear off, an all!'

'You're the one who needs to scarper,'

'I'll have your guts for garters!' screamed Sadie, enjoying herself.' Unnoticed, Jake was slowly circumnavigating the room.

'What's this infernal racket!' boomed the man, who now burst into the room.

'Sorry, Mr Greville, we don't know who they are; they just arrived unannounced,' stammered one of the clerks. They all were quite horrified by the situation but also secretly enjoying it. None of them cared for their master, who overworked and underpaid them. His arrival was a cue for the two girls because, until this moment, they did not know what Robert Greville looked like. Now they could increase the intensity of their onslaught.

'Oh Bobby, Bobby! How could you leave me all alone for so long,' implored Charlotte.

'Robbie!' spat out Sadie, 'What are you doing with this…this…strumpet! You said I was the only one!'

'But, but, I've never seen these women in my life before,' spluttered Greville, addressing his employees.

Jake heard very little of what happened next because he slid through the door to Greville's office and gently locked it from the inside. He knew that Charlotte and Sadie were the only people who would have noticed him because everyone else's eyes were on them. Quickly Jake got to work. He took off his glove and pressed the button on the back of his hand to activate the screwdriver. A twist of his finger ensured it was set to turn anticlockwise, and in a few moments, the motor drive released the two screws fastening the window lock. Then Jake slid open the sash window and with the sharp blade on his ring finger, he scored a cross on the outside of the window frame. He closed the window and, with the mechanical pincers, snipped off the screw heads. He then repositioned the window catch and popped the screw heads in place. No one would realise that the window, which looked locked, could now be opened very easily. Jake opened the door a fraction and peeped out. He could see that the girls were now tussling with each other, commanding the full attention of the horrified Greville and his fascinated employees, so Jake slipped through the door, crossed calmly to the other side of the room and waited. The girls had seen him.

'Do you know what? You can keep him!' shouted Charlotte, and she turned and flounced out of the room.

'I wouldn't touch him with a bargepole!' yelled Sadie, and with one hand on her hip, she too left the office. She couldn't help but ruffle the hair of the youngest office boy, who had been open-mouthed throughout the episode. It was then that one of the clerks noticed Jake, who had waited to make sure the girls left safely.

'Disgraceful!' Jake retorted, then he too left and caught up with Sadie and Charlotte, who were trying their best not to laugh. They lasted until a few steps clear of the building, when all three broke down into hysterical laughter.

Both Jake and Charlotte were involved with the second phase of the plan. Oliver, Billy and Joshua had collected the airship from Blackwall, and now Charlotte had taken over the controls of the Rebel.

'Good, it's a dark, cloudy night,' whispered Jake as he and Joshua descended via a long rope dangling in front of Haddon House. Jake felt round the window frame and located the cross he had scored into it. He transferred his weight onto the stone sill and then prised up the sash. He wriggled through it, followed by the massive bulk of Joshua, who had a little more difficulty squeezing through. Joshua had two roles, firstly, to light and hold the oil lamp, and secondly, to be there as a bodyguard in case they were disturbed by a night watchman. Jake had seen the filing cabinets that lined the room on his visit earlier that day and hoped that Greville would want to keep important information close at hand. Jake searched methodically and neatly. He didn't want any evidence of their visit to remain. At last, he found what he was looking for and stuffed the manila folder into a bag, then he and Joshua left the same way they had come. Jake even balanced the broken lock in place and shut the window carefully so nothing looked amiss.

'Well done, boys,' said Charlotte once Jake and Joshua were back inside the gondola. 'I'm rather hoping that Oliver has resisted the temptation to drink too much so he is sober enough to put the Rebel to bed in Blackwall, and I can tuck myself up in bed at the hotel. It's been a long, hard, but successful day. We can read through the file tomorrow, but right now, Sadie and I have bridges to build after the fight over our failed romances with Robert Greville.' Sadie, who had come along to keep Charlotte company, joined in with the laughter as the Rebel slid through the clouds away from Chancery Lane.

CHAPTER FIVE

The Rebel Runaways were taking tea with Edward at the Majestic Hotel.

'Those were tasty cakes,' said Billy, licking his lips, 'I think they've got the edge over my rock cakes.'

'I think rocks have the edge over your rock cakes,' quipped Sadie.

'I agree, Billy. I'll have to take you for afternoon tea at Twinings, and you can see how it compares with here at The Majestic,' said Oliver.

Edward had been studying the folder Jake and Joshua had 'liberated' from Greville and Wynne.

'This makes for interesting reading,' he said.

'We left the room as we found it,' said Jake, 'So if they go looking for it, with a bit of luck, they will think they have just misfiled it.'

'So now we know the name of the ship, HMS Deception, and it will already have set off, taking a cargo of cloth and cooking implements to Nigeria. Then, the insurance records state it is taking ivory and palm oil to America. But of course, we know otherwise,' said Edward.

'Slaves!' said Joshua bitterly, 'They are putting my people in chains.'

'How long would it take the Rebel to fly to Africa, Oliver?' asked Charlotte.

'I would guess around forty hours, depending on headwinds. Oh, quiet now. Here comes the waitress.'

'My compliments to the chef,' announced Billy. The waitress smiled, glanced over her shoulder and whispered:

'Actually, he doesn't make them himself. We buy them from the City Bakery Store.'

'Well, delicious all the same,' laughed Oliver, 'So nice to be in a civilised establishment once more during these difficult times.'

'Oh no!' sighed the waitress, seeing the door open, 'It won't be civilised for much longer. It's the Golden-Lane gang. They waltz in here, demand free food and insult our diners.' Two youths, wearing hats decorated with gold ribbon, swaggered into the cafe, grabbing cakes off people's plates and tossing them at other diners. They sat at an empty table; one tipped his hat down over his eyes and put his feet on the table.

'It's deadly dull here, ain't it?' he announced, and pretended to go to sleep, making exaggerated snoring noises. Charlotte leant over to Sadie and whispered:

'Rearrange these words: bull, red rag, Oliver.' Sadie did not have time to reply because Oliver immediately sprang to his feet and strode over to the two youths.

'Don't you know it's bad manners not to take your hat off indoors?'

'Wot's it to you, granddad?' came the reply. Oliver's response was to flip the youth's hat off.

'And as for putting your feet on the table, that's beyond reproach!' Oliver shoved the other youth's boots so hard that he fell backwards off his chair, landing with a yell and a crash on the floor. 'I would suggest, gentlemen, that we continue this conversation outside.' Oliver turned and left by the rear door. He didn't bother to check if the louts were behind him. He had insulted them; he knew they would be.

The rest of the Rebel Runaways got up and followed the two gang members to the Majestic's back yard where Oliver, who had discarded his jacket, stood in readiness. He had rolled his sleeves up, he was smiling, and his eyes were twinkling.

'I don't fink you know who you are messing wiv, granddad,' said one of the youths. 'We are the Golden-Lane boys.'

'Allow me to introduce myself. My name is Oliver Moon, and I am a Rebel Runaway,'

'Wot? Like in them stories? I fawt they was made up!'

'No, let me reassure you that I am very real.'

'Well, let me see if yer run away from this,' leered the thug, and he snatched an empty lemonade bottle from a nearby crate and smashed it against the wall to make a lethal weapon. Oliver merely raised an eyebrow and continued to smile. The youth crouched low and approached Oliver. It was then that the other one noticed the onlookers, in particular, the massive frame of Joshua.

'You stay out of it,' he warned.

'Of course. I am only here to see the rules are

observed.'

'Rules?' said the youth with the bottle incredulously, straightening up to look at Joshua. 'Rules? In a street fight?' Two seconds later, Oliver landed an enormous blow on the youth's chin; he crumpled to the floor, sending the bottle spinning on the flagstones.

'Don't be ridiculous, Joshua. There are no rules in a street fight!' scolded Oliver.

For a big man, Joshua was surprisingly light and quick on his feet, and he raced forward and grabbed the second youth from behind, trapping his arms.

'Sorry, my mistake. No rules,' said Joshua.

Oliver polished the end of his right fist with his other hand and drew his arm back. Charlotte gave a gasp of horror and the youth winced, expecting a punch such as he had never experienced before, but when Oliver swung at the youth, he stopped a few inches from his face and simply tweaked his nose, then removed his beribboned hat.

'A moment, Joshua,' said Oliver crossing the yard and lifting the lid off a big metal bin. Oliver had guessed its contents. It was the pig swill bin, where the staff dumped all the leftovers from the hotel kitchen to be collected by a pig farmer at the end of each month. Sadie wrinkled her nose in disgust at the rancid odour. Oliver scooped up a generous portion of the evil mixture with the hat, returned to the youth, and jammed it on his head. 'The only reason you are not out cold, like your companion, is that I want you to be aware that should I, or any of the other Rebel Runaways, encounter you or any of your gang here again, we will chop you up and add you to the pigfeed. Today, you can go in whole.' Oliver promptly swept the struggling youth off his feet, and he and Joshua carried him over to the bin and stood him in it. The foul stew came up to his knees. 'Think yourself lucky we didn't put you in head first! I suggest you leave by the back gate into the alleyway and drag your companion out there with you.'

'Billy, are you sure you feel confident about doing this?' asked Jake.

'Sure, everyfink went smooth as silk when I sneaked into the Steam Works before.'

'I would do it myself, but I would be too easily recognised, whereas you, now you've taken off all your finery and are wearing that brown overall...'

'I know, I look ordinary.'

'Today, ordinary is good. You can look like a peacock tomorrow. Now, remember, the one person in Fotheringay's Steam Works who might recognise you is the supervisor, Grimes, so keep a lookout for him.'

'How can I ever forget him,' said Billy, screwing up his face, 'The ear he twisted still hurts just at the thought of it.'

'Here is the block of soft wax that Maggie made for me when I ordered more candles. Put it in your inside pocket so your body warmth will keep it supple.'

Fifteen minutes later, as the factory bell rang out, Billy nestled himself in the centre of the crowd of workers entering the Steam Works to start their shift. Once inside, he made his way to the engineers' storeroom, where Jake had told him he would find an oil can with a long spout. Then it was a case of remembering Jake's instructions so he could find the Design Room.

'When you get there, the designers will be at work, and the door will be closed but not locked. The key will be on the inside of the door. At the end of the shift, the chief designer will lock the room and take the key to the porter's room. Whilst the factory runs all day, every day, the designers only work until six o'clock, so you should have plenty of time.'

Billy found the room, knocked on the door and opened it.

'Maintenance!' he sang out, then he took the key out of the lock and poured a generous amount of oil into the keyhole. With his back to the room, where everyone was ignoring him anyway, Billy took out the block of wax and pressed the key into it so it made a deep impression. He then replaced the key in the lock, closed the door and walked back the way he had come feeling pleased that his mission had gone so well.

Then, disaster! On the main corridor, a man exited a room. He was reading a document, so he didn't see Billy until he bumped into him.

'Mind where you are going,' he growled. Billy's initial reaction was to think the man should watch where he was going until their eyes locked, and with a tremor of fear, Billy realised that he recognised him. It was Grimes! It took the supervisor a few seconds longer to identify Billy, and then his eyes widened.

'You!' he exploded, but by then Billy had dropped the oil can and fled down the corridor. It wasn't premeditated, but that instinct worked in Billy's favour because as Grimes attempted to give chase, he slipped on the oil, and landed flat on his back. It gave Billy a few valuable seconds to put some distance between himself and his enemy. Billy dodged through a doorway. 'Stop, you little runt!' roared Grimes, and stumbled after him.

Billy found himself in a small passageway leading to a set of stairs. He had no alternative other than to go up. As he reached the first floor, he heard Grimes below. Billy tried the door on the landing, but it was locked. The stairs carried on upwards, so he had to continue his ascent. Grimes was a much stronger man than Billy, but he wasn't very fit, and Billy began to increase the distance between them as he continued to climb, trying doors on the way. He prayed there wouldn't be a locked door at the top because, if he was forced to go back down, there would be no way he could get past Grimes.

Luckily there wasn't a door, locked or otherwise, at the top of the stairs. Instead, the landing opened out into a series of long rooms filled with broken and discarded items. Billy dashed through room after room. He could tell, by the slope of the ceiling, that he was in the roof space, and then he noticed that each room was crossed by a beam of sunshine in which danced particles of dust. Skylights!

Billy clambered onto a packing case and flipped the catch on one of the skylights. It opened and he squeezed through onto the roof. It was a scary prospect, but so too was the thought of Grimes, who he could hear searching through the first room. Billy closed the skylight after him, but now he had nothing to hold onto, and he started to slip down the roof. He was too shocked to call out, for he knew he wouldn't survive the fall. Billy slid down the slates on his back - all he could see was the sky, the clouds and the sun. He wondered whether, if he got to heaven, he would be able to look down on this rooftop. Perversely, he was also pleased that the block of wax was in his inside top pocket and wasn't getting squashed. Then suddenly, his feet made contact with something solid, and he stopped. If the roof had been constructed so that the guttering was fixed below it, Billy would have slid straight off it to his death, but this building had a low parapet around it with a stone gutter inside, and that was where Billy had come to rest. It took him quite a few minutes to recover his composure, then very carefully, he twisted around so he was kneeling in the gutter and peered over the side. He held on tightly as a wave of nausea overtook him. It was so high up. Then he saw one of several iron downpipes connected to the guttering. What was significant about this one was that it passed only a few inches from a cast iron staircase several feet below. So, this was where all the locked doors led to - a fire escape that would be inaccessible in the event of a fire! Billy noticed that fixed to the roof, in line with the fire escape, was a wooden ladder leading up to the ridge of the roof. That was odd. Perhaps it had been left after chimney repairs, but anyway, it was down he wanted to go, not up. Billy edged along the roof's edge and swung his feet over to grip the downpipe. Then he slid the few feet down until he made contact with the fire escape and safety.

'Hello, Billy,' said Jake, who was waiting for him, 'You're early; the factory bell hasn't gone yet. I didn't expect you to come from that direction either.' Billy told Jake about his narrow escape as they walked to Old Nick's foundry. 'I know those attic rooms!' cried Jake. I had to dump stuff up there once. If you had kept on going for two or three more rooms, you would have found another staircase going down.'

'Oh no! Now you tell me. I went through all that for nothing!'

'No, no! Firstly, Grimes would assume that you went out that way. He wouldn't realise that anyone would be daft enough to climb through a skylight.'

'I fink "brave enough" would be a better way of putting it.'

'Anyway, that gives me a way of getting into the building. I could go up the fire escape, climb that wooden ladder you noticed, shimmy along the ridge tiles and then drop down to the skylight. What's more, if I had my Tool Kit hand fitted, I'm sure I could manage to pick the lock on the top door from the inside; no one would dream it was open, so getting in and out of the Steam Works will be easy from now on and, once Old Nick has cast a new key from the wax mould you made, I will be able to get into the Design Room too, so I can keep tabs on what Fotheringay is up to. Well done, Billy!'

CHAPTER SIX

'I like it when you lot get in my boat, cause I gets to 'ave a little rest,' said Craggs, the boatman. Joshua looked up from the oars and smiled.

'I've been doing nothing other than sitting around for a long while,' he said, 'My muscles were starting to get flabby.'

'Oh! Ere we go! It's the Navy. I 'ope you've got yer Thames Permits,' said Craggs.

'Our what?' asked Oliver. 'I don't know what you're talking about.'

'Surely yer know about the permits? They just started this week. Yer gotta 'ave a permit to travel on the Thames.'

'Why? That's ridiculous. The river belongs to everyone.'

'Everyone can look at it, but yer need permission if yer wanna travel on it. It's pretty obvious why. It's 'cause of all the 'orses dyin'. More and more people' ave been usin' the river to travel, and 'cause yer 'ave to be able to write to fill in the application form, it means that the posh folk can 'ave the river to themselves. The army don't need 'em, of course. They can pretty much do wot they like. Oh, look lively! I can't outrun 'em. They are fast, these ketches.' The two-masted Navy sailing boat drew alongside them.

'Papers!' demanded the Naval Officer standing in the bow.

'Jake,' whispered Sadie, 'Can the 'Glove' work underwater?'

'I suppose so, maybe just for a few minutes.'

'That's all I need,' she replied, slipping the weapon onto her hand. 'Distract them, Oliver, she whispered, 'Make a fuss!' Oliver was only too pleased to oblige. By now, the Naval Officer had inspected the boatman's permit and demanded to see Joshua's. A stream of Mandinka greeted him as Joshua pretended not to know English and hurled every insult he could think of at them in his native African language. Then Oliver stood up, making the boat rock alarmingly.

'This is an outrage! .... Meanwhile, Sadie reached over the side of the boat. No one was watching her in all the commotion, and once the Glove was submerged, she aimed it at the ketch and pulled the trigger. She quickly pulled her arm back, not wanting the water to get into the workings.

'Sit down, and shut up!' shouted the Naval Captain.

'Sir!'

'Not now!'

'But. Sir. We are taking in water. There is a hole in the

starboard hull and another in the port,' persisted the Midshipman. 'If we don't head for the riverbank, we might sink.' The thought of getting his crisp white suit wet in the filthy brown river made the Officer abandon all thoughts of checking permits, and without another word from him, the ketch made for the riverbank.

'Well done, Sadie,' said Oliver, 'Quick thinking!'

'I'm impressed that the dart shot in one side and out the other,' said Jake.

'I don't reckon they are too pleased about it,' laughed Sadie; the ketch was now sinking dangerously low in the water.

'In Manchester, we would say that the Captain had the mulligrubs now that his fine white suit is all wet and muddy.'

'Mulligrubs! That's a good word!' said Billy.

'Aye, it means to be in a bad mood.'

'Yer means he's got his bleedin' dander up!'

'Cor blimey!' cried Billy, furiously waving out of the window and jumping up and down in excitement, 'Anuvver bloomin' airship! We ain't never clapped eyes on one o' them before, an' it's 'eadin' our direction!'

'Erm, I don't mean to curb your enthusiasm, but it's not necessarily a good thing,' observed Oliver.

'Why not,'

'You see that roundel painted on the nose? That means the airship belongs to the Air-Fleet, and we are none too popular with the military right now after our escapade with Fotheringay's cannon.'

'What will they do?' asked Charlotte.

'Hopefully, they will want to talk and not shoot us

down,' replied Oliver. 'I imagine that, ideally, they will want us to surrender the Rebel.'

'Will we do that?' asked Jake with concern.

'Hell no!'

'Can we outrun them?' asked Charlotte from the helm.

'Unfortunately not,' replied Oliver, 'Well, not in a straight race. Theirs is a lighter and faster craft, but with Jake's alterations, we have more short-term thrust. I have a plan, but first of all, I'll go to the door and see if they want to talk. Keep the Rebel hovering, Charlotte, and listen for my instructions. Billy, make sure the clockwork motor drive is fully wound and remain at your post. You may have to do a lot more winding shortly.' Oliver opened the gondola's door and waited for the Air-Fleet's craft to draw alongside.

'Oliver Moon! We have been sent to escort you back to the base.'

'Is that you, Curby?' yelled Oliver.

'Yes. I mean no, I am Wing Commander Curbishly. I repeat, you must follow us.'

'Promoted, eh? You are doing well for yourself Curby'

'She's fully wound now,' called Billy.

'Good work, Billy,' replied Oliver. 'So it's Curby. He was a sweet boy but not the brightest star in the sky. Let's see if we can confuse them. Charlotte, on my command, I want you to make the Rebel drop vertically as fast as you can.'

Oliver continued his conversation with Curbishly: 'Spot of bother with the engine, I'm afraid. We keep losing height.' They were near enough to see the smug look on Curbishly's face as, not knowing about Jake's alterations, he clearly thought that Oliver's airship was an antiquated model.

'Just follow us and try to keep up,' shouted Curbishly.

'Now, Charlotte! Drop!' cried Oliver. The speed they descended made Sadie give an involuntary scream. 'Stop, and now engage the thrust motor and take her hard to starboard; we are going to fly right underneath them. They won't be sure where we are.' Oliver leant out of the door and looked up to locate the Air-Fleet airship. 'We are clear. Now take her up as quickly as you can, faster than you have ever flown before. Billy, wind like hell!' The Rebel shot up, passing the other airship as it climbed high into the sky. 'I don't think anyone saw us, I can't be sure, but they were probably looking out the other side. Now, take us back to port, Charlotte. I want you to keep the Rebel directly above theirs. They definitely can't see us now. Their envelope will obscure the view. Mimic whatever they do, Charlotte. We are safe up here.'

'Are we going to blow them out of the skies?' asked Joshua.

'Nothing so dramatic. Apart from the fact that if they exploded, we might catch a spark and go the same way, I am aware that these chaps are just obeying commands. I served with some of them. I think a small leak is more in order. Joshua, It's time to try out the Gauntlet. But you'd better tie a rope to the harpoon. If you miss your target, we don't want it to hit someone on the ground. How are you doing, Charlotte?'

'I'm fine; I'm quite enjoying it. It's very windy, though, so I have to keep my wits about me. I've taken the thrust motor off now. It's back to gentle movements.'

'I could tell you a story about thrusting and gentle movements, but maybe now is not the time,' laughed Sadie. Oliver raised an eyebrow. Sadie's joking masked the fact that she was very nervous. Charlotte could see it in her eyes. She beckoned to her friend.

'Come up here and keep me company, Sadie.'

Joshua now had his Gauntlet on his arm and secured a rope to the harpoon, which he tied onto the gondola.

'Fire at anywhere in the envelope,' said Oliver, pointing at the balloon below them. Joshua took aim and the harpoon shot through the air, but it was caught by the wind and veered sideways, missing its target. Jake hauled the harpoon up again, and Joshua reloaded, but again it missed. He tried twice more before Jake interrupted:

'It's no good. It's too windy. I think it's time I tried out my new hand and also tested the improvements I've made to the winch.' Jake pulled off a cover to reveal the winch fixed to the deck near the door. It was obvious that Jake had made adaptations because an assembly of shiny brass cogs adorned the exterior of the reel. Jake picked up the harness fastened to the end of the cable. 'Can someone do up my straps?'

Joshua obliged: 'Is that tight enough?'

'Ouf! I can hardly breathe. Joshua, you don't always have to use your full strength for every task, you know! Right, my new hand, The Dart, is fitted. The winch is easy to use. No muscles are required. Billy, you can operate it.'

'Cheek! I'll 'ave yer know that me muscles are proper well-developed for a boy of my age.'

Jake grinned. 'When I'm outside, twist the lever to the left, and I'll descend. With the lever in the middle, the winch will stop and I'll come back up when you turn it to the right.'

Sadie shuddered as Jake climbed out of the door.

'It still makes me nervous getting in and out of this thing,' she said. Billy twisted the lever, and Jake began to drop. He spun wildly as the wind caught him, so he curled up into a ball to try and combat it. Oliver knew Jake was attempting to land on the airship below and shouted instructions to Charlotte, who couldn't see him.

'Three degrees to starboard, reverse, stop...' Finally, Jake made contact with the airship, bouncing on its envelope. He only needed a few seconds. Kneeling on the balloon, he placed The Dart against it and pressed the trigger button on the back with his other hand. He couldn't miss. Then, feeling the stream of hydrogen whistling against his face, he sprang away, arcing into the air and spinning in the wind. Billy knew this was a signal to turn the lever and bring Jake back to safety.

'Nothing dramatic will happen. They will lose altitude gradually,' said Oliver, then turning to Charlotte, he said, 'Stay directly over them and take the Rebel up, so when they finally reach the ground, we will be in the clouds and long gone! Good work, crew!'

Sunlight streamed through the window of the Westminster office. Maybe it was his experience as a tactician on the battlefield, but Field Marshal Bellings always preferred to sit with his back to the sun. He felt that making everyone else squint and struggle to see him properly gave him an advantage. Since the army seized power, the stakes had never been so high, so he needed to exploit any opportunity to assert his dominance. He was chairing an exclusive meeting to get an update on security matters.

'Major Blackford, please apprise me of the current situation in London.'

'We are in control, but only just. As you know, we have relinquished our authority in certain lower-class areas such as The Rookery.'

'The slums, you mean,' interjected Bellings.

'Yes, Sir. They aren't exactly no-go areas, but we have to tread carefully, arrive in force and be sensitive to the fact that the street gangs have the power in these areas. That's not to say that they don't have an influence outside those districts, because shopkeepers throughout the city complain that the gangs extort protection money from them. At first, the fire brigade was busy dealing with an extraordinary number of fires, but that has died down now as shopkeepers have learned that it is better to pay up than risk having their premises burnt down in retaliation.'

'This alliance between the London gangs; is that still holding up?' asked General Truscott.

'Yes, it is. On the one hand, it makes them all-powerful, but on the other, at least the situation is fairly stable. We know what we are dealing with.'

'We may need to give some thought as to when and how we should break up that alliance,' said Bellings.

'We have ordered the Bow Street Runners and the police force to concentrate their efforts on protecting the more well-heeled areas in the city, so-called Toff Town, for instance. As you know, this government needs the support of the affluent. Initially, when horse flu took its toll, many fled to their country estates, but more and more of them are returning.'

'And the country as a whole, Truscott?'

'As with London, it's stable but on a knife edge. We maintain control of the railways and have commissioned more third-class carriages at the expense of the second-class so that we can transport troops around the country effectively in the event of any unrest. The Navy has authority over all the waterways, requiring permits to be purchased by crew and passengers, from the simplest rowing boat on the Thames to the largest barge on the canals. Apart from bringing in revenue, it has cut down on congestion and ensured the more important citizens can get from A to B without having to walk.'

'Tell me about the situation in the prisons, Ridgley.'

'Not surprisingly, given the increased poverty and lack of food throughout the country, more people are turning to crime. There has been an upsurge in petty theft, so our prisons have been filling up fast, and conditions are pretty dire in there. However, in every cloud, there's a silver lining, Sir, and we are requisitioning prisoners to do much of the work that horses used to do. We have to deploy a few armed soldiers as guards, of course, but it's amazing what loads a chain gang can pull and actually, they prefer to be out on a working party than stuck behind bars. Fresh air and better food!'

'Can anyone throw any light on the Rebel Runaways? I keep seeing stories about them - penny dreadfuls - being sold on the streets.'

'They are very popular amongst the working classes, Sir,' replied Truscott, 'And very elusive too. I don't doubt that some of the stories are works of pure fiction, but reports in the press corroborate some of the Runaways' exploits. Reuters, for example, often feature stories about them, and such is the influence of that agency, using the telegraph service to distribute news, that these stories represent an undoubted threat to our authority.'

'Where are they based? You can't make an airship disappear into thin air! Surely it doesn't live permanently in the clouds?' asked Bellings.

'We don't know, Sir. We have agents working on it. Fotheringay's man, Hastings, has prioritised it too. There are repeated sightings of them in Bristol, so maybe they are somewhere in Somerset or beyond.'

'The Air-Fleet will have to redouble their efforts to track them down. I don't know what they are playing at!' barked Bellings. 'Now, this may come as a surprise, given what you have said about our relationship with the street gangs, but I want one of the gang leaders picked up; It doesn't matter which one. I don't want him damaged, though. It goes without saying we should seize any opportunity to pick off members of the Rebel Runaways. Theirs is a chapter we need to close...for good!'

CHAPTER SEVEN

To most Londoners, now the age of the horse was over, this was a familiar sight, a working party of prisoners, chained together and pulling a large handcart guarded by soldiers. Each step was accompanied by the rhythmic beat of chains warning the pedestrians on the busy street to give way. Only those familiar with London's underworld would recognise that one of the convicts was none other than Crusty Jack, the leader of the Black Feathers street gang, and only the most observant would notice some odd behaviour; a relay was taking place. A man would exchange a few words with Crusty Jack before speeding ahead, only to be replaced by another man. When the working party caught up with the first man, he and Crusty Jack would continue their conversation. This process was repeated several times.

Later that afternoon, a group of senior members of the Black Feathers assembled in a back room of The Executioner, the pub that served as their headquarters.

'Right! I fink I got all the conversations with Crusty Jack assembled in the proper order,' announced Crooked, who had assumed temporary leadership of the gang, 'It would 'ave 'elped if some of yer could write and also remember in wot order yer spoke to 'im.'

'So wot's' e say then? Are we gonna spring 'im from Newgate Prison or grab 'im when 'e's on a workin' party?'

'We ain't gonna do neiver,' growled Crooked, "E's done a deal wiv the soldiers. 'E reckons that's why they lifted 'im in the first place. The gov'ment wants 'im to do their dirty work. They'll drop all charges in return for exchangin' 'im for one of our 'ostages.'

'Wot 'ostages? We ain't got no 'ostages!'

'Not yet, we don't, my friends,' replied Crooked with a leer, 'But we will 'ave.'

Billy whistled as he walked through the alleyways in The Rookery, heading back to the hotel. He had been chatting about courier pigeons all morning with his new friend, Bert, and had picked up many useful tips and tricks. He knew to look out for soldiers; their bright red coats made them hard to miss and easy to avoid. The street gangs were another matter. They lurked in the shadows and could appear in an instant. Billy had already paid a toll to one of the Black Feathers on his way into The Rookery. It was a strange experience because the gang members usually paid little attention to their victims, but this one had looked him up and down, from his top hat decorated with cogs and a set of goggles down to his shiny leather boots, and given him a lopsided smile.

'Must be impressed with my stylish threads,' thought Billy proudly, puffing out his chest and sticking his thumbs into the pockets of his richly embroidered waistcoat.

Billy was resigned to paying another toll because the same man, joined by three other Black Feathers sprawled on a handcart, was blocking the path ahead. As Billy rummaged in his pocket to find a coin, an outstretched hand stopped him in his tracks. He was aware of movement from the man's companions, when suddenly all went dark; an overpowering smell of hessian filled his nostrils and he was upended and thrown onto the cart.

'Billy's been captured!' gasped Edward, rushing into the hotel room where he had arranged to meet the Rebel Runaways, then doubling up, out of breath, 'I ran all the way here.'

'Who's got him?' cried Joshua, rising and clenching his fists.

'Calm down,' urged Oliver, 'Just tell us what you know, Edward.'

'Word came through to Reuters. The Government released a statement saying they have one of the Rebels in custody and that he has been tried and found guilty of treason and will be publicly hanged at Newgate Prison in the morning.'

'But how...?' stammered Jake.

'Rumour has it that Field Marshal Bellings did a deal with the Black Feathers. Anyway, what can we do? There's bound to be a show of force by the military, both in the prison and in the air. They probably want to flush you out.'

'Oh, we'll be there alright,' cried Oliver, banging his fist on the table, 'One thing you can depend on, we'll be there!'

'The gods are with us,' breathed Oliver as he prepared to descend on the rope ladder swinging from the Rebel. 'It's a cloudy night, no sign of the moon. I'll go first, then Jake, Sadie and Joshua. Charlotte, please follow us and pick us up at the far end of the field.'

'If we are successful tonight,' thought Jake, as he dropped to the ground, 'I bet the Air-Fleet will stop keeping all their airships and balloons in the same field.'

When the four were assembled on the airfield, Charlotte took the Rebel higher in case the guards spotted it and fired in her direction. Oliver put a finger to his lips, reminding them they had to carry out the operation in total silence. He pointed first to Joshua and then to a row of airships tethered to a gantry running along the far side of the field. Joshua untied his Gauntlet and harpoon, which had been slung behind his back, and sped off. A double line of balloons, of various shapes and sizes, ran the length of the field. Some were inflated and tethered, while others were draped over the side of their baskets, waiting to be filled with hot air once the crew had lit the brazier. Oliver gestured for Jake to tackle the balloons flying on the left and for Sadie to deal with those on the right. He himself would concentrate on the balloons yet to be inflated. Jake had descended with his Dart hand already fitted, and now Sadie slipped on the Glove and ran across to take her position, while Oliver drew his sword. Then, silently, the campaign began.

Joshua fired his harpoon at the first airship. One shot.

It would have been hard to miss. Then he pulled on the rope securing the harpoon, catching it before it hit the ground, reloaded, and moved on to the next. The theory was that, with a single shot, the airships would slowly deflate and the gondolas would come to rest against the gantry gradually rather than crashing into it. It was vital not to alert the guards. So far, it seemed to be working.

Sadie and Jake passed from one balloon to the next, firing into the underbelly, knowing that the darts would pierce the balloons on the way in and out. Meanwhile, Oliver dashed from one hot air balloon to the next, slashing and stabbing. It took all his self-control not to let out a war cry as he did so. Finally, the four assembled close to the gatehouse at the far end of the field. They turned to survey the damage they had caused. The entire Air-Fleet was grounded. Oliver waved his sword to signal to the Rebel, and Charlotte brought it down until the rope ladder was within reach.

'Idiots!' laughed Oliver as they recounted their mission to Charlotte, 'You would think that, given they are the Air-Fleet, it might occur to them that danger might come from the skies. Still, we can't be too complacent in the future; they will learn from their mistakes. Well done, Jake, your weaponry worked astoundingly well!'

'Ah well,' thought Billy, sitting in a Newgate Prison cell, *'It looks like this is the end of the bloomin' road. It's all been a bit of a whirl, really; one minute, there I was, strollin' through The Rookery, and the next I was tied up in a sack and delivered into the 'ands of the soldiers. I was 'auled in front of some military court. It only lasted a few minutes. The judge says, 'Do yer deny that yer a member of the so-called Rebel Runaways?' Well wot else could I say other than: 'Yes,*

I am, and proud of it' and that was bleedin' well that. They shoved me into this cell. At least I'm on me own. I saw some of the other cells, and there were dozens of geezers crammed into each one. I could 'ear 'em wailin' and shoutin' and cussin' all bleedin' night. Shocking. Made it very difficult to get any kip! Maybe they didn't want me smart togs to get messed up before the mornin's big event. It might tarnish their reputation if people saw I 'ad been knocked about. Pity, I lost me top 'at somewhere along the way.

'So, wot do I fink? If I 'ad the choice to go back in time, I'd do it all again. I've seen more, done more and learned more since I met Mr Moon than I did in all me bleedin' life before, not to mention the new mates I've made. So would I swap a long life, scrabblin' in the gutter like a bloomin' rat, for a short one flutterin' in the sunshine like a flamin' butterfly? Well, wot d'you fink? Not on yer Nelly!

Ave I got any regrets? Well, I've been learnin' to read and write proper, but I 'ave a little more difficulty wiv long words. Me spellin' ain't so good. So I would 'ave liked more time to get all that better. Also, anyone who knows me now will tell ya that I love grub and I love cookin'. There are loads of dishes I've read about on menus that I dunno 'ow to make. So it's regrets abaht what I ain't done rather than the stuff I 'ave done!

'Old on. Sounds like they're comin' for me. I 'ope there's a good crowd. I'd 'ate to leave this earth without anybody noticin'!'

'Awright, awright!' yelled Billy as he was shoved roughly out of the prison gate and sent tumbling into the dusty courtyard, 'No need fer that!' Billy climbed the wooden steps up to the gantry, dusted his clothes off, and then looked in amazement at the sight before him. The square was jam-packed with spectators. Surrounding the crowd, he could see a cordon of soldiers holding muskets. The onlookers cheered when they saw Billy. 'I wonder, are they pleased to see me, or do they want to see me swing?' Billy looked up at the gallows behind him and decided that now was the time to mask his nervousness with bravado. He stepped to the front of the platform, waved, and performed an elaborate bow. The crowd roared their approval. 'They are wiv me!' Billy smiled until one of the three soldiers guarding him shoved him back towards the gallows. The spectators booed. The fourth man on the platform, dressed in black, was the hangman, and he grabbed hold of Billy and tied his hands behind his back. He dragged him back a few steps so he was standing over a trapdoor.

The executioner forced a noose over Billy's head and pulled it tight. Billy stared out at the crowd, determined not to show any emotion. At first, he was puzzled, for many in the crowd appeared to be waving papers above their heads; then, he smiled in recognition. They were copies of Edward's 'Chronicles of The Rebel Runaways.' 'A rebel to the end!' yelled Billy, and the crowd cheered. The next surprising thing was that suddenly, everybody was looking up. The reason for this was apparent to him a few seconds later when Oliver slid down a rope and landed on the platform beside him, swiftly followed by Sadie, who jumped off a rope ladder and lastly, Jake. Billy looked up and saw the familiar shape of the Rebel. Joshua was lying on the deck, aiming his Gauntlet down below.

The hangman lunged towards the lever that would open the trapdoor and send Billy to his death. Before he could do so, in one swift movement, Oliver drew his sword, spun around and sliced through the rope above Billy's head, so the noose hung limply on Billy's chest. The hangman stopped, realising there was no longer any point in opening the trapdoor, and fearing for his own safety, he leapt off the back of the platform and fled towards the security of the prison.

It was as though the soldiers were awakened from a trance, and one of them raised his loaded musket and aimed it at Oliver's head. He never got a chance to squeeze the trigger because Sadie had already trained the Glove on him, and a metal dart pierced his heart. As he crumpled to the floor, the second soldier was shouldering his gun to fire. Jake aimed his Dart hand, but Sadie got there first, and that man, too, fell to the floor. The third soldier looked at his comrades and decided that retreat was the best option. He dropped his musket and leapt off the platform as energetically as the hangman.

Oliver stepped behind Billy and cut the ropes binding his hands. Billy then eased the noose over his head and flung it into the crowd, who responded with a deafening roar. They surged forward and were now so tightly compressed that they formed an impenetrable barrier between the cordon of soldiers and the gallows. As the soldiers let fly a volley towards the platform Oliver said:

'Take a bow, my friends; it's time to leave.' So, as the Rebel Runaways took their curtain call a barrage of shots flew well above their heads, accompanied by clapping and cheering from the onlookers. Only one soldier had thought to aim at the airship. He stepped back, dropped to one knee and raised his gun. Joshua had been waiting for this moment and released a harpoon. He would have been lucky to have found his mark from such a distance, and the harpoon thudded into the ground a few feet from the soldier, but it was enough to scare him, and the soldier disappeared into the safety of the crowd.

As soon as everyone had a foot on the ladder or was clinging onto the rope, Charlotte took the airship higher, well out of the reach of any musket balls. Once everyone was aboard the Rebel, Sadie smothered Billy with kisses, and there was back-slapping all round. Edward was feverishly making notes. He had no doubts about the subject of his next story, and he was determined that with the help of his printers, it would be for sale on the streets the very next day.

Later that evening, Charlotte and Sadie were talking in the hotel room. Billy was fast asleep as he hadn't slept the night before, and the others had taken the Rebel back to its hiding place in Blackwall.

'How do you feel, Sadie?' asked Charlotte.

'What do you mean "How do I feel?"'

'I saw you kill two people at Newgate Prison. I know that if you hadn't, those soldiers would have killed one of us, but how does that make you feel?'

'To be absolutely honest, if you want to know how I feel inside, the answer is one word - nothing!'

'Really?'

'It's hard to explain, it was as though I had switched to my former self, when I was a child and used to imagine I was someone else, so the things men were doing weren't happening to the real me. I sometimes did the same thing when I worked at Madame Boo Boo's, and it was the same when I sorted out those two Edinburgh villains. They had such low regard for me as a person that I felt no more emotion than I would if I were wiping a speck of dust from my eye.' Charlotte rushed around to hug Sadie.

'Oh, Sadie! You've had such a hard life.' Sadie rested her head on Charlotte's shoulder.

'That was then, and this is now, and I am as happy as

can be but I will kill anyone, without a moment's thought, that tries to harm any of you.'

CHAPTER EIGHT

'You've done a good job wiv them papers.' Craggs nodded his approval as he studied the Thames Water passes on the journey to Blackwall.

'Courtesy of Edward's printer and Jake's expertise in forging signatures,' replied Oliver. The Rebels always sought out Craggs now to transport them up and down the Thames. By paying him double the usual fare they knew that they were guaranteed discretion should the authorities question him about his passengers. It was an arrangement that suited Craggs, too. Apart from the extra money for the journey, Oliver had made an investment enabling Craggs to purchase another, much larger boat with a sail, which was just as well, for today his passengers had brought far more luggage than usual, including a handcart. Moreover, Craggs rarely had to do much work because Joshua was happy to do all the rowing.

The journey passed without incident. If the Rebels had encountered the Wild Boys, Oliver would have paid them off so as not to attract any attention, but it was too early for any gangs to be up and about. They would have been sleeping off the beer funded by the previous day's tolls. However, as the Runaways neared the hidden home of the airship, Charlotte gave a gasp because she was the first to see around twenty men sitting on wooden crates with their backs to the tunnel entrance, obviously waiting for them. Sadie reached for her Glove, but Oliver held up a restraining hand.

'Don't worry. Those men are my friends. I didn't mention them before in case they didn't turn up, but by the looks of it, they are all here. They are all retired sailors. I spent a lot of time in the company of this grizzly crew on a long trip to India when I was in the army.' The sailors sprang up to greet Oliver.

'Aye, we drank a lot of rum on that trip, didn't we?' laughed one of them.

'I can see you've brought your essential provisions, Jinks,' replied Oliver, gesturing to the crates and joining in with the merriment.

Charlotte looked at Sadie and rolled her eyes in exasperation. The last thing that Oliver needed now was the company of old pals with a bountiful supply of rum.

'Gentlemen,' said Oliver, 'Although perhaps that's a misnomer. Allow me to introduce you to the Rebel Runaways, Charlotte - our pilot, Jake, Sadie, Joshua and Billy. Also with us is our secret Rebel, Edward, who immortalises our exploits in print. He has a vivid imagination! So, let's get our ship airborne. The first stop is

Bristol, where Jake wants to pick up even more cogs and springs and heaven knows what else.'

'It's going to be a long trip. I need to be busy,' said Jake.

'And I've gotta pick up enough grub to last us. We don't wanna get scurvy, mate!' said Billy.

'Don't you worry. We can survive on bully beef and ship's biscuit,' laughed Jinks, 'And rum, of course!'

"We come on the sloop John B.,
My grandfather and me,
Around Nassau town we did roam.
Drinking all night,
Got into a fight,
Well, I feel so break up,
I want to go home."

'How many more times are they going to sing this shanty?' groaned Sadie.

'It doesn't exactly set a good example for Oliver,' replied Charlotte, at the helm. 'Drinking all night! At least he's not fighting!'

"So hoist up the John B's sails,
See how the mainsail sets,
Call for the Captain ashore,
Let me go home,
Let me go home,
I want to go home,
Well, I feel so break up,
I want to go home."

'Keep your eye on Oliver, Sadie, will you?' asked Charlotte, 'I know he's enjoying himself, but you might remind him that he has to take over the helm from me in a couple of hours so I can get some sleep. There's a lot of rum-drinking going on back there!'

'I don't know how you do it, Charlotte. You've been standing there steering the Rebel for hours and it was the same yesterday. Don't you get bored? It's not as though there's owt interesting to look at through the window! Everything is yellow.'

'That's the Sahara Desert,' chipped in Jake. He had come to the front of the airship to check the navigation maps. 'Just one degree to starboard, Charlotte.'

'To answer your question, Sadie, no, I never get bored. Sometimes I almost feel that I'm riding on the wind outside the airship. The lift we get from the thermals here, over the hot sand, is very different from when we are flying over the ocean, for instance. I feel all those weather conditions through these levers and the wheel. I do believe that Oliver flies the same way - by instinct.'

'Let's hope his instincts can navigate through a sea of rum!' laughed Sadie. 'Ah, another shanty. I don't think I've 'eard this one for at least an hour!'

> "*Oh, blow the man down, bullies, blow the man down*
> *Wey hey, blow the man down*
> *Oh, blow the man down, bullies, blow him away*
> *Give me some time to blow the man down!*"

'Wake up! Wake up!' shouted Sadie, shaking Oliver

out of his drunken slumber. Oliver groaned. 'You've got to clear your head.'

'Where are we,' he growled in a voice so deep and rasping Sadie felt it could have cut through solid wood.

'We've crossed the northern half of Africa, leaving the Ivory Coast behind us, and now we are zig-zagging over the South Atlantic Ocean,' called Charlotte.

'We think the HMS Deception will have set sail from The Gambia by now with its human cargo, so it's just a simple case of spotting her in this vast ocean,' added Edward.

Oliver noticed everyone else was awake and stationed at windows around the gondola, scouring the seas.

'I thought you were hitting the bottle a bit hard last night,' grinned Nathan, one of the sailors, and he began to sing:

'And it's all for me grog, ye jolly jolly grog.

All for me beer and tobacco.'

'No more sea shanties,' snapped Charlotte. 'We've got work to do.'

'Aye, aye, Captain!' Nathan smiled and returned to searching for the slave ship.

Oliver doused his head in a bucket of water, then approached Charlotte sheepishly.

'Erm, did I miss my shift last night?' Charlotte looked steadily ahead and nodded.

'Very sorry about that.'

'Are you in a fit state to take the helm now so I can catch up on some sleep?' The chastened Oliver grabbed the wheel, giving Charlotte the chance to get some rest.

'No more sea shanties,' she repeated before falling asleep.

She awoke to hear Billy shouting:

'There it is! There it is!'

'No,' replied one of the sailors, 'It's only got two masts; the one we are looking for has three.'

'I know. Not that one, be'ind it, on the 'orizon.'

'By God, he might be right,' exclaimed the sailor, putting a telescope to his eye. 'Well done, matey! She's worth a closer look.'

Twenty minutes later the Rebel was hovering directly over the ship that Billy had spotted.

'Aye, that's the Deception, all right,' announced Nathan, 'I sailed on her once as a lad.'

'Good! What's the plan, Oliver?' asked Jake.

'Quite simply, we go down and ask them to turn around and return the slaves.'

'Is that it?' asked Jake, 'But what if they don't?'

'Ah, then we can give them the option of getting in the lifeboats and leaving the boat to us,' replied Oliver.

'And that's where we come in,' said Jinks.

'But, why should they give us the boat?'

'We will just have to be very persuasive,' replied Oliver with a smile.

'At least there are a few more of us,' Sadie interjected.

'Oi, we ain't going aboard unless the ship has been abandoned; otherwise, we would be pirates,' asserted Nathan.

'Oh, give me strength!' sighed Jake, 'And don't look so pleased about it, Edward. I know what you're thinking - another adventure for one of your books!'

'Good afternoon,' called Oliver brightly as he slid down the rope.

'Good afternoon,' echoed Jake. For a moment, the

sailor in the crow's nest thought his heart had stopped. It was bad enough being sent high up the mast to scan the horizon for pirates - every roll of the ship was magnified up here and he felt seasick - but he hadn't thought to look directly upward; why should he?

'Good afternoon,' said Sadie as she passed him. He knew he should call out, but a wave of nausea overtook the astonished sailor, and instead, he was sick over the side of his barrel-like perch.

A few seconds later, Oliver, Jake, Joshua, Sadie and Edward were assembled on the deck of HMS Deception. Oliver held up a white handkerchief.

The first to see them was a young deckhand who dropped his scrubbing brush into his tin pail of water in surprise.

'Please could you alert your Captain to our arrival?' asked Oliver. The boy took another look at the visitors; his eye followed the rope up to the airship hovering above them and then he rushed off in the direction of the bridge.

Five minutes later, the Captain, the first and second mates and the bosun confronted the Rebel Runaways.

'What's the meaning of this?' demanded the Captain. By now, a straggly group of sailors had encircled the visitors, all extremely wary because they had never had an encounter like this before.

'Sir, we have simply come to request that you turn your ship around and return your cargo whence it came.'

'How dare you!' blustered the Captain, 'This is my ship, and I will not take orders. Silas, show these trespassers what we are made of.' A tall, muscular sailor holding a large hammer approached, then, singling out Oliver as his target; he let out a roar and rushed at him. Unfortunately for him, the one person that he had disregarded as being unimportant was the most deadly. Sadie's glove was already primed and she pulled the trigger. She intended to aim for the man's heart, but at that moment the ship rolled and instead, the dart pierced his throat. It stopped him all the same and Silas fell to the floor, gurgling and clutching his neck.

'Show us what you are made of, you say,' said Sadie, her voice flat and calm, 'It appears that you are made of flesh and blood. Rather too much blood, I think.' She stepped forward and fired another dart into the writhing man's head, and all movement stopped as the life left his body.

It was striking that not a single member of the Rebel Runaways had flinched during the attack.

'Gentlemen, please remember, we came under a white flag wishing you no harm,' said Oliver.

'Perhaps I could interject,' offered Jake. Oliver smiled to think of the contrast between this eloquent young man and the stumbling, shy lad he had first met. 'No doubt you may be wondering what might happen should you not turn around,' continued Jake, 'Let me introduce you to the Spider.' Jake put his hand in his pocket and withdrew a sphere about the size of a small apple made of brass and steel. 'But first, imagine this: a dark night and most of you are asleep when we fly above you and drop a dozen of these.' Jake tossed the sphere in the air and it landed at the Captain's feet. On impact, eight legs emerged from the metal ball, and it proceeded to spin.

'Hah!' snorted the captain, 'A child's toy!' The whole crew was laughing now but the laughter stopped when the Spider withdrew its legs and dropped through the hole it had cut in the deck.

'I don't know what is below us, but perhaps I should

inform you that once it makes contact with the next deck, it will cut a hole in that and so on until it drops through the hull into the ocean, and the sea will rise up to greet you. I imagine that it won't take long for this ship to sink. So, with that in mind, I think you should send someone to retrieve the Spider. Be careful - it's sharp.' Jake emptied the water out of the deckhand's bucket and handed it back to him.

'Go!' screamed the captain, and the boy scampered down the hatch in search of the Spider. The crew murmured uneasily amongst themselves. Eventually, the deckhand reappeared, with the Spider noisily clattering around in the bottom of the metal pail. Jake deftly reached in and pressed the concealed button, making the Spider turn back into a ball.

'So just imagine dozens of these raining down on your ship every night. The stuff of nightmares!' said Jake. Actually, this was a bluff because he only had three Spiders.

'But if you did that, the, erm, cargo would perish.'

'I can speak from personal experience,' said Joshua, stepping forward. 'I remember the hardships of the voyage in a slave ship like this one. The pain and the heartache - I wouldn't wish that on anyone. But that's just the start of the journey. Afterwards, there is cruelty and inhumanity. Many times I wished I was dead. Far better to sink below the waves and, in a few moments, meet your gods with your African soul intact.'

'I need to confer with my men,' said the Captain, thoroughly convinced by Joshua's assertion that he was prepared to let the slaves drown.

'Certainly, Sir,' replied Oliver. 'We will take in the view from the bow.'

'A fine piece of acting,' whispered Jake to Joshua. 'I know you would do anything to try and save your fellow

Africans.' Joshua allowed himself a fleeting smile.

There was much dissent amongst the Deception's crew.

'I say we rush 'em.'

'I fear they are alive to that possibility,' replied the Captain. 'I see now that at least three of them have some kind of monstrous weapon. I, for one, do not want to be on the receiving end of a spike. And for God's sake, somebody throw Silas's body overboard! No, I think we call their bluff. We man the lifeboats but keep the Deception in our sights. After all, these five people couldn't sail a boat like this, well four if you discount the filly. I predict they won't have a clue and will simply fly away. Mischief-makers are what they are.'

Thirty minutes later, the entire crew of the Deception climbed down into four lifeboats, carrying enough food and water for five days. They watched their ship drifting aimlessly and struck out with the oars. They needed to put some distance between themselves and the Deception, but not too much as they were certain they would be returning to take control shortly.

'That's far enough. Hold! Square your oars in the water,' commanded the Captain. The Deception was now a distant silhouette. The men in the lifeboats were too far away to notice the twenty sailors shinning down ropes from the airship. However, they couldn't help but see that someone had expertly trimmed the ship's sails. The Deception cut an arc through the waves and headed East towards Africa.

CHAPTER NINE

Joshua shimmied up the rear mast with the mooring rope that Charlotte had lowered from the Rebel and secured the airship to the Deception. Now there was no need for a pilot; the ship would tow the airship, so Charlotte and Billy joined the others on the deck. The sailors who, when aboard the Rebel, had seemed to Charlotte to be an unruly rabble had now become a well-disciplined crew. Each knew their role, and they relished being in control of a large sailing ship again. Charlotte didn't even mind hearing the sea shanties as they hauled the great sails into place.

Billy's first port of call was the galley, and he was delighted to see the provisions aboard, ready for a long sea voyage. He hadn't been able to cook whilst on the Rebel, and now he seized the opportunity to rustle up one of his speciality stews.

Charlotte joined Jake, Oliver, Edward, Sadie and Joshua.

'It's time we ventured down to the lower deck,' said Oliver, 'Joshua, are you ready for this?' Joshua nodded, 'Then you lead the way. It's fitting that the first face they should see is a fellow African.'

With great trepidation, they climbed down the ladder to the belly of the ship. As they reached the deck where the slaves were, Joshua froze. He had completely underestimated the effect of being back in these conditions and wave after wave of fear and nausea overtook him. Sadie immediately spotted what was happening and she jumped off the final rung of the ladder and put her arms around Joshua to comfort him. Then she gasped as her eyes adjusted to the dark. Four rows of African men and women were chained to the deck, and together with the stench and the moaning and wailing, it was no wonder that her friend had been transported back to the horrors of his first journey on a slave ship. Joshua took a deep breath.

'I'm fine now, thank you,' he said. He strode over to a door. It was locked, so he kicked it in. He knew what he was looking for. He emerged from the storeroom with a large bunch of keys and went straight to the nearest man. Joshua's hands were shaking as he struggled to find the right key. When the manacle sprang open, the effect was unexpected. The man pushed past everyone to reach the ladder and climbed up into daylight, followed by Joshua and Sadie. Much to the bemusement of the sailors, the man was wildly dashing from one side of the ship to the other, looking for a means of escape.

'Please, stop. We won't hurt you,' shouted Joshua,

speaking in Mandinka. Luckily the slave understood him and paused, looking warily at Joshua and Sadie. 'You are free now, but you must return to the others. You won't be chained up, and we will bring you food.' Joshua gestured to the frightened man that he should follow. Sadie followed suit, then sensing that she needed to do more to coax him back, she stepped towards the slave, took him by the hand and led him to the hatch.

Back on the lower deck, Charlotte took control.

'Before we free anyone else, we must first explain the situation to them. If they all rush up to the deck, there will be mayhem. We could sound the ship's bell every thirty minutes so a group of, say, twenty-five could go up to the deck to get some fresh air. Tell them, Joshua, that we will bring food. I don't mind helping swill the deck down. It's disgusting that they have been made to lie in their own filth. Find out if any of them are ill - we will isolate them, so diseases don't spread.' Joshua nodded his agreement.

'One other thing,' added Oliver, 'Find out if anyone knows of any African towns or villages where they build boats or ships.'

Charlotte called into the galley to see Billy. A pot was bubbling away on the stove.

'A right old tasty stew will be comin' in your direction in abaht an hour, and don't you worry; I've whipped up enough for the crew as well..'

'Erm, I hate to break it to you, but you've forgotten about our guests in the hold. We need about four hundred extra portions.' Billy's face fell. 'I think you will need some assistance; Sadie and I will join you. You can tell us what to do. There are women amongst the slaves; maybe they would be willing to help. They might teach you a thing or two.' Billy now beamed in delight. This was the closest he had ever been to having his own restaurant.

It turned out that Sadie and Charlotte didn't need to help as there were five women who were only too happy to join Billy in the galley. The deck soon reverberated to the sound of singing and laughter. Far from being the head chef in charge of a restaurant, Billy soon found himself as very much the commis chef, the junior. He didn't mind, though; he loved the atmosphere created by these dynamic women even though he didn't understand a word they said. They appeared to berate him for the poor choice of vegetables and lack of spices on the ship, and try as he may, he couldn't communicate that it wasn't his fault. However, it was all good-humoured, and Billy relished the opportunity to look and learn.

'Well, you might as well,' said Charlotte, 'When will you ever be this close again?'

'Do you think he will mind?' asked Joshua.

'I'm certain he won't mind. Anyway, it will be me piloting the Rebel, and I think it's a good idea. The seamen have just discovered the Deception's supply of rum. No doubt he will be helping them dispose of that once we have finished with the ship.'

'How long until we land? We've been hugging the coastline for some time now.'

'Nathan said we will be there in a couple of hours. It's a town that is a centre for shipbuilding.'

'I know it,' replied Joshua. 'There is a lot of very useful timber in this ship. They will be able to strip it all down and wood that isn't suitable for ships will be used for houses. I imagine they will have a festival of thanks for our gift.'

'I can guarantee that if there is eating, drinking and dancing, the Rebel Runaways will be there!' replied Charlotte. 'Come, let's go and ask Oliver.'

Later that day, Joshua went down to the lower deck. The atmosphere was so different now. The Africans had rearranged themselves to sit in tribal groups and now beat rhythms on the wooden floor, drumming in a call-and-response fashion. Joshua switched to speaking in Yoruba, the language of his homeland.

'Is anyone here from Yorubaland?' A group of six men stopped drumming and stood up.

'Come to the top deck, please.' When they were assembled outside, Joshua continued, 'I am Yoruba too. As you know, we will land soon and set everyone free. Some may choose to stop and settle in that prosperous place, whereas others may try and attempt to walk to their own villages and towns. This ship will be broken up, and after that, the crew will return to travelling in the Rebel.' Joshua pointed up at the airship tethered to the mast. 'What I am about to tell you has to be a secret. Before we return to England, we will visit the Yoruba village where I am from, near Oyo. We would have enough room to take you with us.' Their broad smiles clearly indicated what they thought about that idea!

'My wife, Bisi! She is working in the kitchen,' said Damola.

'We have room for her too. As I said, it must be a secret because we can't take everyone back to their homelands.'

'Tell me, Joshua, what is your African name?' asked Damola.

'It's a long time since anyone called me this. I am Abiola Okoro'

'Really? I am also an Okoro. Maybe we are cousins.'

'You shouldn't feel disappointed, Joshua. I knew halfway through the party last night that Oliver wouldn't be coming with us,' said Charlotte early the following morning, 'There are two sides to Oliver; the polite, charming man, and once the drink takes him, there is his rumbustious, devil-may-care twin, always a hair's breadth away from kissing you or fighting you. There is no way of controlling that version of him. Eventually, sleep overtakes him, which wipes out the next two days. So, even if we got him aboard the Rebel, he would be a liability. It's nothing personal, Joshua.' Joshua nodded, and then he smiled.

'That was some party last night, wasn't it? I haven't danced to African rhythms for such a long time.'

'We were very impressed. Thankfully, Billy has learned from his experience in Bristol when he drank too much and mostly stayed with the women in the galley. He says he has added many more dishes to his repertoire.'

'I saw Damola teaching you how to swing your hips when you dance,' chuckled Joshua.

'I know!' said Charlotte blushing, 'In Bristol, they taught me how to dance Irish jigs, but this was altogether something quite different!'

'Tonight, the town is having another party in celebration of how successful last night's party was,' said Joshua.

'They will have to stop celebrating sometime soon,' said Charlotte, 'They have to get the Deception completely stripped of everything useful, and then they have to tow it out to deep waters and sink it. If the British arrive, there must be no trace that the ship was ever here!'

It was early afternoon before the Rebel Runaways gathered in the clearing where Charlotte had tethered the airship. Joshua asked one of the newly freed slaves to keep an eye on Oliver whilst they were away. His reward for keeping him out of trouble was the promise of one of Joshua's leather belts, which had an oversized, decorative buckle shaped like a snake's head. The sailors stayed to help dismantle The Deception, something they could do even in a constant state of mild intoxication. Whilst the seven Yorubas who would travel in the airship were now used to the sight of it hovering above them, they found the prospect of actually getting aboard absolutely terrifying. Charlotte and Jake climbed the rope ladder first. Jake started the clockwork engine, while Charlotte kept the Rebel steady.

'Don't look down,' instructed Joshua as Damola warily climbed the ladder. The others gave a cheer as he reached the gondola. No amount of encouragement could persuade his wife, Bisi, to follow him, so Jake lowered the harness he had fastened at the end of his clockwork-operated reel. Billy, who was by now almost like a son to her, helped fasten the harness around her. She thought that it was just a safety precaution whilst she climbed the ladder, but Jake had other ideas. Once Billy had given him a thumbs-up, he pressed the start button on the reel, and Bisi was hoisted up into the air, wriggling and screaming, accompanied by roars of laughter from her compatriots. Once she was safely inside, the other Africans climbed the rope ladder, with just a little prodding from Joshua, followed by Billy and Edward. Joshua cast off the ropes tethering the Rebel to the ground, and as soon as he had set foot on the rope ladder, Charlotte flicked the levers to make the airship rise. She was keen to take off before anyone got cold feet and changed their mind about coming.

She need not have worried. Everyone gathered around the windows, taking the opportunity to see their homeland from a different viewpoint. When flying in Britain, Charlotte often stayed above the clouds to ensure the authorities could not chart their progress. However, that did not matter here, and Charlotte flew as low as she dared. When they had come from England, much of the journey across Africa had either been above an unchanging Sahara desert or at night. Now was her opportunity to see a changing landscape as steamy jungles gave way to plains and savannah.

'Now we have reached the grasslands, we are getting closer to my home,' said Joshua.

'Cor blimey! Wot the bleedin' hell are them strange fings?' cried Billy.

'I know what they are,' replied Charlotte. I've seen them in books, but I never thought I would see one in real life. They are giraffes and look over there - elephants!' Once, they followed a group of hunters trying to track a herd of antelope. Joshua translated Damola's remarks for the benefit of the crew.

'He says those hunters have more chance of swallowing the moon than killing one of those antelope. They have broken from their cover too early.' Sure enough, as the hunters rushed forward, the antelope took flight. It was then that the hunters noticed the airship and vented their anger by throwing spears at it. They fell harmlessly to the ground as the Rebel flew three times higher than a man could throw.

'That gives me an idea,' said Joshua, 'Billy, help me

into the harness.' Shortly afterwards, Joshua said to Charlotte: 'Can you see that herd of buffalo over there? Please can you take us just above them and fly a little lower?'

Charlotte obliged and was thrilled to follow the buffalo as they stampeded across the plain. Then, after giving instructions to Jake, Joshua climbed out of the gondola, and Jake lowered him until he was a few feet above the beasts.

Charlotte was so intent on steering the airship that she failed to notice that Joshua was wearing his Gauntlet. He fired a harpoon, piercing one of the buffaloes through the neck, and it crashed to the ground. Joshua had purposely not secured the harpoon with a rope because he knew the forward movement of the airship would have dragged him from the ladder. Joshua waved to Jake, who had already shouted to Charlotte to stop and winched Joshua up to the gondola to excited applause and cheering from the other Yorubas. Charlotte was horrified.

'What have you done?' she gasped.

'I have killed a buffalo,' he replied proudly.

'But why? They are beautiful.'

'For the meat. It is our tradition.'

'It's your tradition to hunt animals from airships with harpoons, is it?'

'Well, no, but these are modern times. Please can we go back for it? It will be a gift for my village.'

'He's got a point,' said Billy, 'You ate my beef stew happily enough the other day.'

'Well, don't ask me to do that again,' Charlotte said sniffily, 'And it's not coming in here. You can fasten it to a rope, and it will have to dangle below us. Poor thing!'

For years to come, the residents of Oyo talked about

the day an African buffalo steered a magical flying machine into their town and then lay down in the marketplace to sacrifice itself for a magnificent feast. As well as seven other Yorubas from nearby villages and towns, the buffalo brought back their very own lost son, Abiola Okoro, sometimes known as Joshua.

'It has grown,' said Joshua to the Oba Jaja, the royal chief of Oyo. 'When I was taken into slavery, it was just a village, and now look at it! Your palace is magnificent.' The Rebel Runaways were sitting in a circle in the Oba's house and were breaking and sharing kola nuts, a traditional symbol of welcome and hospitality.

'It is such a pity that your parents are no longer alive to see you return, but you have your sister and her family.'

'I am looking forward to seeing my sister, although she was a baby when I was last here, so I hardly remember her.'

It's hard to believe that the white men came this far into Africa to capture slaves,' commented Charlotte.

'Oh, you are mistaken,' said Joshua, 'It's not white men that captured slaves; it's other African tribes at war with us. It has always been like that, but what the white man created was a bigger demand, so the African slave traders would take the men and women they captured to the coast and sell them to the Europeans. It's a wicked trade, and I am proud that I have played a part in rescuing some of my kinfolk from its evil clutches.'

CHAPTER TEN

The Rebel Runaways settled down for a good night's sleep, exhausted by the evening's festivities. Sadie and Charlotte were sleeping in the hut of the chief's third wife. The others, sleeping on bamboo platforms, shared Joshua's cousin's home. They had been asleep for less than an hour when a dreadful wailing pierced the night air. The whole compound emptied from their huts to find Adunni, the second wife, on her knees, shouting and screaming.

'She is saying that men came in the night, bound and gagged her, and took her daughter, Jibola. She has only just managed to free herself,' translated Joshua. 'Jibola is my cousin.'

'What can we do?' asked Charlotte. 'Maybe the Rebel will be helpful.'

'Not to start with because the kidnappers will be in the jungle and you won't be able to see anything through the trees, but later, if they cross the plains or travel up the river, it may give us an advantage.' Tayo, one of Joshua's cousins, came running up to him.

'Abiola, have you heard?' he gasped, 'They have taken Jibola! It's most certainly men from inland. Adunni heard them speak and recognised the dialect.'

'Yes, we will be ready to leave in a few minutes. I will go on foot, and the others will search from our airship,' said Joshua. Tayo shook his head and replied to Joshua, who translated it for the benefit of the others. 'He says they can't go yet. The Elder has gone to consult the Oracle.'

'The Oracle?' asked Edward.

'Yes, the priest relays the commands from the oracle. They will never defy it.'

'The priest?' asked Sadie in surprise. 'You mean the Jesuits are here?'

'No, our Yoruba priest. Our religion is ancient and has many customs and traditions. I hope the priest is quick.'

It was probably only half an hour, but it felt like a lifetime before Tayo came running back.

'We have to assemble thirty of our strongest warriors, which sadly won't include me, and set off at dawn.'

'Dawn!' exploded Joshua,' That will be too late. We've lost so much time already. I'm not duty-bound to follow the Oracle. My friends and I will go now.'

'Please wait a moment,' said Tayo, and he rushed away again. Five minutes later, he came dashing back with a big smile.

'I can go with you. I explained to the elders that you were leaving shortly to look for Jibola, and I asked if I could accompany you to protect you from the evil spirits in the forest, and they said yes!'

'You? Protect me?' laughed Joshua, giving him a playful box around the ears. 'Have you a spare machete? We have a couple of good oil lamps from the Rebel with us.' Then switching to English, he told the others the plan. He and Tayo would head north on foot, and the Rebel crew should look out for the light from their oil lamps dancing in the night sky, which would signal for someone to descend for instructions. If they were still searching by daybreak, they would light a bonfire and, by dampening it, send a stream of smoke into the air as the signal to meet them. Once it was light, the Rebel could find the river and scan for boats carrying the raiders.

They were ready ten minutes later. On the Rebel, Jake, Sadie, and Billy attempted to catch up on sleep whilst Charlotte and Edward served as pilot and lookout. On the ground, the adrenaline pumping around Joshua's veins banished all thoughts of sleep as he and Tayo entered the jungle, following the path the raiders were likely to have taken.

'They won't have stayed on this path for long because it just leads to another village,' said Tayo. 'We must look for signs of where they have left it.'

'Look! There!' said Joshua shortly afterwards, pointing to a broken branch above his head.

'Abiola, you have been away too long! Unless they are riding giraffes, I would say a monkey broke that. It's too high!' A few minutes later they saw signs that someone had trampled the undergrowth.

'Here!' exclaimed Tayo, examining the spot, 'This is recent.' Suddenly Joshua was startled by the sound of crying, but it sounded more like a baby crying than an adult. A baby, here in the middle of the jungle? Then he relaxed.

'I have been away a long time,' he thought. 'Of course, it's a bush baby.' Tayo, though, was far from relaxed.

'Quickly, let's go. They are evil spirits and can kill people.' Joshua smiled. He noticed the timid little saucer-eyed monkeys leaping from tree to tree behind Tayo. He had been afraid of them too when he was young, but not now. Joshua quickened his pace anyway. The raiding party had a big head start over them. Mind you, he and Tayo daren't travel too fast for fear of missing the trail and couldn't risk tripping in case their oil lamps blew out.

After a while, Joshua placed a hand on Tayo's shoulder to halt his progress and put a finger to his lips in what he hoped was a universal signal for silence. He pointed into the undergrowth, from where he had heard a noise, and beckoned for Tayo to follow him. Tayo shook his head in disbelief but followed all the same. Joshua thought to himself:

'I don't know how many there are, but at least we have the advantage of surprise.' Joshua crept silently through the jungle with his machete raised high. Surprise was undoubtedly a factor in what happened next, as Joshua was bowled over by a stampede of startled bush pigs. Despite their agreement to remain silent, Tayo couldn't help himself and doubled up, roaring with laughter.

'I could hear that they were bush pigs, my friend. You have been away too long!'

In the sky, the crew were not having any better luck.

'It's too dark!' said Charlotte, 'I can't see anything through the trees.' Eventually, they spotted a change in the terrain.

'I think that is the river down there,' said Edward, 'But it's so black that we won't be able to see if there is any activity on it.'

'I'm very tired,' complained Charlotte. 'The best thing I can do is take us up a little higher and set the motors to hover. We should be fine as long as the wind doesn't change much. Then if the rest of you take turns at the helm, I can nap while we wait for daybreak. Keep an eye on the view out of the window and wake me if it changes radically.'

'Look!' Joshua and Tayo were jogging along a well-trodden path, 'Someone has left this track recently,' said Tayo, pointing to the disturbed undergrowth. They followed the signs and arrived at a circle of flattened jungle plants with another path leading away from it. 'I know what has happened. I smell water. I think the river must be near, and they dragged their boat and hid it here before coming to our village. We must follow that path, but if it does lead to the river, I fear they will have long gone and we will have no chance of catching them.'

'Don't forget, the Rebel Runaways are on your side.' Joshua could see by the expression on Tayo's face that he thought that was unlikely to be an advantage.

Five minutes later, they were standing on the bank of a wide river. Tayo was gloomy and muttered miserable oaths to himself.

'Look on the bright side,' said Joshua, 'At least we can see the sky; let's wave our lamps to see if we can attract the others.'

'The only things we will attract are evil spirits.'

'The sun will come up soon and banish all those evil spirits that you are so afraid of. Then, if they haven't seen our lamps, we can light a fire and send a message in smoke.'

Charlotte was woken by Sadie gently shaking her shoulder.

'It's morning,' she said. 'I think we have drifted a little

but haven't lost much height. Billy has spotted smoke coming from the riverbank. It might be Joshua and Tayo.'

Once those on the Rebel had located the men, they lowered the rope ladder.

'Tayo won't come,' sighed Joshua as he climbed through the door. 'He thinks the Rebel is a messenger from the god of thunder and lightning, Shango, and that we should first sacrifice a goat and make a stew of okra with shrimp and palm oil.'

'I'm willing to try cooking that,' said Billy brightly, 'If you could tell me where I can get some shrimps and what okra is!'

'I've told him to stay by the fire,' continued Joshua, ignoring Billy's not-very-helpful offer, 'The warriors from the village will have set off by now. They are sure to track him. He can tell them we have gone to find the raiders' boat.'

'Which way?' asked Charlotte, springing into action.

'North. Upstream.'

'It's a long way to come just to get a wife,' remarked Edward after they had been travelling at full speed for an hour.

'The raiders will see it as a test of their manhood,' replied Joshua. 'If they succeed, they will be awarded titles within their tribe and gain power and wealth. There will be a great feast, and their village will sing songs about them for years.'

'So the girl herself is immaterial,' snorted Sadie in disgust.

'Only in as much as she is the daughter of an important man.'

'Your face is a picture, Sadie,' laughed Charlotte, 'How angry can one girl look?'

'Men!' spat Sadie as she resumed her post as lookout. Almost immediately, she shouted, 'There, look! A boat!' Edward trained his binoculars on a long canoe.

'I think this is them,' he shouted, 'There are six men paddling, but I am sure there is someone tied up at the back.' Sadie immediately fetched her glove, and Joshua got his gauntlet ready.

'Steady now,' warned Jake, 'You can't go firing darts at them. You'll risk hitting Jibola. We need to be cleverer. Who did you say the god of thunder and lightning was, Joshua?'

'Shango,'

'They won't have seen us because they are facing the other way. Charlotte, you take the Rebel as low as you can, and when we are in shouting distance, Joshua, you pretend to be Shango and tell them to paddle to the bank and leave Jibola there,' instructed Jake.

In theory, it was a good plan. However, Jake had underestimated just how fearful of the god the kidnappers were, and when they heard Joshua's voice booming out and saw the airship bearing down on them, instead of obeying instructions, they all leapt into the water and struck out for the river bank, leaving Jibola to her fate.

'Oh no!' shouted Billy. He pointed to one of the swimmers who was making very slow progress and then to a long, dark shape languidly slipping into the water.

'It's a crocodile!' yelled Joshua, arming himself with his gauntlet.

'Must you keep killing animals?' asked Charlotte.

'If I don't, it will kill that man.'

'Can't you just, I don't know, distract it or something?'

'I'll try, but if it doesn't cooperate, it will feel the sharp end of my javelin,' gasped Joshua as he began to climb down the rope ladder.

The canoe bearing Jibola stopped and slowly spun around to begin travelling downstream.

'Sadie, please can you keep an eye on the boat? As long as Jibola lies still, she should be alright,' said Charlotte.

'At least that will occupy Sadie so she doesn't feel inclined to fire darts at people,' thought Jake to himself. Meanwhile, Joshua was at the foot of the ladder, between the crocodile and the swimming raider, and he began to splash the water with his feet. He attracted the crocodile's attention, which surfaced and powered towards him. Joshua realised he needed to retreat up the ladder at about the same time the crocodile realised its prey was within reach. As Joshua climbed, the crocodile launched itself in a massive vertical leap and snapped its jaws shut. If Charlotte had not slammed the boosters on a few seconds earlier to take the Rebel higher, Joshua would have lost a foot. As it was, the crocodile's jaws snapped shut on the ladder itself, and as the Rebel rose, so too did the thrashing reptile. It was an impasse: Once the crocodile had something in its jaws, it wasn't inclined to let go. Joshua scrambled up the ladder and shouted into the gondola.

'Pass me a sharp knife.'

'Don't kill it,' commanded Charlotte. Joshua simply smiled in response. Charlotte was following the drifting canoe at a distance. The last thing she wanted was to drop an angry crocodile on top of Jibola. Joshua descended and peered at the beast. He prodded him with the knife. The crocodile growled and stared back, its eyes angry and red, but it held fast. Then Joshua got to work with the knife. A few moments later, they all heard a splash as the crocodile dropped into the river.

'Is it alive?' asked Charlotte.

'Very much so,' replied Joshua, 'But I'm afraid we have lost the last few feet of the rope ladder.'

'Quick,' called Sadie, 'The canoe is starting to rock.'

'Take me down,' commanded Joshua, 'I'll paddle the canoe back. It will be easy to travel downstream.'

'I'll help,' said Edward.

The canoe arrived back to where Tayo was waiting at the same time as the village war party arrived. The riverside resounded to joyous whooping and singing as Jibola was reunited with the villagers.

'You will be pleased to know, Billy, that I heard one of the elders instruct another to make sure they tell the women to get a supply of shrimps and okra so it looks like you might get to taste that stew after all,' said Joshua. 'Let's get Shango here back to the village and we can tell them the good news.'

CHAPTER ELEVEN

'What a feast that was, Abiola!' said Oba Jaja, patting his stomach. 'You will be a legend in these parts. Warriors will sing songs about your bravery for generations. Can I persuade you to stay with us? We are increasingly under threat since the relationship between the Laderin and the Yamba houses broke down. It's virtually civil war.'

'I say this with a heavy heart, but I have been away for too long to settle back here, and I feel part of a new tribe now. I hope God protects you.'

'Tell me, Abiola, can you bring us horses? We have cavalry but no horses,' asked the Oba.

'Sadly, no. It is the same the world over. The horses have all died.' Joshua kept to himself the fact that a herd of wild ponies had survived the horse flu on Foula. Anyway, a tiny Shetland pony would hardly be a suitable beast to carry an African warrior.

'You look sad, Joshua,' said Charlotte on the journey back to the coast to collect Oliver and the sailors. 'Are you alright?'

'Yes, I am glad I returned. It's like an open wound has healed. Of course I am sad to leave but I feel I'm in the right place with all of you,' replied Joshua.

Joshua didn't express all he was thinking; it seemed disloyal to his countrymen. He knew he could never adopt their beliefs and superstitions again, nor would he have the patience to endure the endless rituals and ceremonies. For some reason, Joshua's thoughts turned to a slave he had known in America. She had been pregnant when she had been captured and later gave birth to twins who had grown up to be fine, healthy young boys. They were fortunate that they had been born into a foreign culture, even though they were enslaved, because if the twins had been born in his village in Africa, they would have been taken out to the jungle and left to die, as twins were considered a bad omen that could bring devastation to their community. Something else he hadn't shared with the rest of the crew was the discussion he had heard about Billy. The men from the village couldn't understand why Billy liked to help with the cooking, 'That's women's work!' Joshua had tried to explain that in the West, many chefs were men, but they didn't believe him. He even heard one man suggest that if Billy were a native of their village, they would kill him as an offering to Obatala, the creator of human bodies and God of moral uprightness. Just as he was thinking about Billy, the boy himself popped up in front of him.

"Ere, ave a butcher's at one of these. Guaranteed to put a smile on yer boat race.'

'I only understood some of that, Billy,'

'Ave a butcher's - butcher's hook - look. A smile on yer boat race - face!'

'Ah! Akara and pap.' Joshua dipped the fried bean cake ball into the fermented corn starch and popped it into his mouth. 'Mmm! Delicious. We used to eat these for breakfast on Saturdays.'

'I made them wiv Bisi; she taught me how to make dodo too.'

'Fried plantain! A wonderful snack,' mumbled Joshua, devouring one.

'It's funny, neither of us could speak each other's language, but somehow, through cooking, we understood each other completely. Now, do you think I will be able to buy cassava flour, yams and ground crayfish on The Old Kent Road?'

'We'll be in England shortly,' announced Charlotte. Rather than fly over Spain and France, as she had on the way to Africa, this time Charlotte had steered a course over the North Atlantic. After negotiating a tricky spot of turbulence shortly after leaving the African coastline, Charlotte crossed the sea to meet the North Atlantic Drift and then made good progress with the winds behind her. 'First stop, Bristol.'

Jake looked up and smiled. Everyone else was asleep.

'You must be very tired, Charlotte.'

'I am. A fat load of good Oliver was on this trip,' she said, 'Permanently drunk or asleep, or both!'

'I noticed you had Nathan steering the Rebel at one

point.'

'Yes, his rum consumption was more moderate, and he was used to being at the helm of a sailing ship, so he picked it up quite well. It allowed me to take a little nap. He had strict instructions to wake me if he got into difficulties, but it was all plain sailing, so to speak! Anyway, what have you been up to all of this journey? You've hardly stopped working. Are those a couple of planks from the Deception's deck?'

'Yes, they are. Wasn't it fun when we saw the remains of the ship sinking? I've decided to call my new invention a mono-scoot. It's going to be a means of transport for one. The wood from the deck is the base, but underneath, there is a clockwork motor drive.'

'Why am I not surprised that you found a way of incorporating clockwork,' laughed Charlotte.

'It has two small wheels at the back, and at the front is another innovation - a single wheel.'

'Will it have a seat?' asked Charlotte.

'I considered it, but I think it will be easier to balance while standing, so I've connected a long handle to the front wheel to steer it. And last but not least, a canister containing compressed steam will be mounted on the back. It's a miniature version of a design I copied in your father's factory when I sneaked in one night. Not only will the steam supply the mono-scoot with a tremendous acceleration boost, but in doing so, it will also wind up the clockwork motor. It's the canister that I am going to pick up from George Adlam & Sons in Bristol.'

'Ingenious!' replied Charlotte. 'When we get there, you can take your time. I'll moor the Rebel up for a while and catch up on my sleep before we return to London.'

'I'm proper excited to see if them carrier pigeons wot I let loose in Africa 'ave made it back safe an' sound to London,' said Billy.

Edward smiled. 'Let me thank you again for letting one of them carry a message with a brief description of you all capturing the Deception. I've never written in such small script. Anyway, that was just a taster; the full report is to come. Do you think your friend will have delivered the message to the Reuters office?'

'If the pigeon's made it back, I'm bleedin' certain 'e will 'ave. 'E's only too chuffed to put 'is birds to graft. 'E's over the moon 'cause since meetin' me in the butcher's, 'is pigeons get to travel to far-flung places wiv us..'

'I'll be giving him a healthy tip if he has passed on my message. It's a strange combination of old and new. Carrier pigeons have been used for over three thousand years, but Reuters' telegraphy is brand new. Putting the two together means that the story might be broadcast around the world long before we get back to England ourselves!'

'You 'aven't hardly stopped writing the whole time on this trip,' said Billy.

'That's true. It's been a perfect opportunity to experience new adventures and get them down in writing. As well as a full report to Reuters, although, of course without naming any of the sailors involved, I'll also be dropping off several stories to my publishers. You can expect some new Chronicles of the Rebel Runaways on sale on the streets very soon.'

'Since I've been learnin' to read and write, I've been keepin' a note of all the different recipes I've learned about. Fancy any for yer booklets?'

'Hmmm!' replied Edward, trying to let Billy down gently, 'I don't think the audience for my adventure stories would be interested in cookery tips. I imagine they would turn to Mrs Beeton's book if they wanted advice.'

'Yeah, but I bet you she ain't got any recipes for African Efo Riro soup or Locust Bean Stew!'

'Erm! You are probably right. Locust Bean Stew. Sounds, ah, delicious.'

'It is. It ain't got locusts in it, though. That's the name of the beans.'

'Anyway, keep up the good work. You never know, maybe one day there will be a demand for recipe books!'

CHAPTER TWELVE

Standing as near to the front as he could get, Edward surveyed the packed room. He was thankful for the tip he had received from one of his sources to come to this evening's meeting. The sun, now low in the sky, streamed through the windows, illuminating a fug of tobacco smoke hanging heavy in the air, which, combined with the odour of sweat, made it obvious that he was in the company of working men. Once, the owners of the Crown Hotel had aspirations that its large upstairs room would be a destination to which London's polite society would flock for genteel tea dances, but the reputation of the hotel had already faded, and now it served mainly as a meeting room. Edward had dressed to blend in. After spending time in the company of the Rebel Runaways, where, although he didn't compete with the extravagant fashions of the group, he didn't look out of place, tonight, he had dressed in old, worn clothes. He watched two men whispering together in front of the stage. He guessed they were organisers because each wore a red sash around one arm. Edward was alarmed when one of them appeared to point at him, but when there was no eye contact, he realised they were identifying someone behind him. Several other men joined the whispered conversation, and then four of them pushed through the crowd to confront somebody.

'We know who you are, Hastings. You're not welcome here. You must leave.' The men took Hastings by the elbows and escorted him towards the door. Angrily, he tried to release himself from their grip, but these were strong men and he did not succeed.

Of course, Hastings! Edward hadn't noticed him. In fact, although Charlotte and Jake had often talked about Hastings, pinpointing him as their arch enemy, Edward had only seen him once before, on the day that the Rebels had thwarted the Steam Works trial of a super cannon. Then, Hastings had started the day the epitome of self-important pomposity and ended it writhing and screaming on the floor with part of his finger missing, caught by shrapnel from the cannon when it exploded.

Hastings was deposited on the pavement outside The Crown and scowled as the door to the Meeting Room was slammed in his face. He wasn't unduly worried. Even though his employer, Fotheringay, had expressly told him to find out what the troublemakers were talking about at the meeting, it was more the affront to his dignity that annoyed him. He knew that there was always a strong possibility that an employee from the Steam Works might identify him; after all, his methods of enforcing order at the factory relied on being highly visible and very brutal. It was for this reason he had not come alone. He had arrived with Tompkins, a distant cousin who was not a Steam Works employee and would not be known to anyone, and they had stood in different parts of the room. Hastings didn't like Tompkins, whom he considered idle and untrustworthy, but then again, Hastings didn't like anyone but himself. However, for a few shillings, he found it very useful to employ Tompkins to keep an ear to the ground and monitor what was happening amongst the working classes, so Fotheringay would still get a report of today's meeting. Meanwhile, Hastings retired to a coffee house to wait.

Inside, the meeting had begun. Edward recognised the man standing at the podium. He was Jacky Storm, a leading member of the growing Trades Union Congress. His standpoint was diametrically opposed to Fotheringay's. Fotheringay was only interested in profit and power, whereas Storm fought to improve the working conditions of ordinary men.

'Friends. We all know that since the horse flu, our lives have got harder and we workers are poorer,' shouted Jacky Storm to the enthusiastic agreement of his audience. 'But it's plain to see. The employers use this flu as an excuse to keep us down and pay us less. I don't see it hitting their pockets! The robber barons are getting richer!' The hall echoed to the sound of stamping feet. Jacky Storm paused for a moment and waited for the noise to subside. 'Do you remember we used to have a democracy?' he said quietly. A disgruntled murmur rippled through the meeting room. 'I know what most of you are thinking: "Well, I don't have the right to vote". It's true! But since the pioneering work of the Chartists back in the Thirties, we in the Trades Union movement have been making progress, and many more of you have been added to the electorate, but now, what have we got? A military junta is using the horse flu as an excuse to rule us and it's got to stop!' Again, the sound of stamping feet signalled approval of Jacky Storm's speech. 'So what do I say we do? We strike. We strike, and we march on Parliament. We say enough is enough, and we demand fair pay and better working conditions! We show them what the working man is made of!'

Jake raised his top hat to greet Maggie, who responded with a giggle.

'Oh Jake. Look at you standing there in all your finery! Come in, out of sight of prying eyes; Not that I mean people will think that you and I are...' her voice tailed off. Jake laughed as he stepped through the door.

'I know what you mean, Maggie. There are many people, Fotheringay and the army generals among them, who would love to see me locked up. More than that. They would have me strung up or standing before a firing squad.'

'Oh! Don't! I can't bear the thought of it.'

'Not that there would be anything wrong with you and I...' Now it was the turn of Jake's voice to tail off as he struggled and failed to find the right words. After an awkward pause, he continued. 'Anyway, I've brought you some money. It's hidden in my boot. Here. It's payment upfront for another shipment of candles. Oliver likes to give them as a gift to the islanders on...on...where we moor the airship when we are not in London.' Jake noticed the look on Maggie's face after his clumsy attempt not to reveal the island of Foula's name. 'Oh, Maggie. Believe me. I don't want to keep secrets from you; it's just that if you don't know where we go, then no one can force you to tell them.'

'I understand,' she whispered, but inside, she was thinking: 'Maybe he doesn't care for me. Perhaps, now he is famous and wears such elegant clothes, he is above a poor working girl like me.' Jake was equally full of inner turmoil. He did care for Maggie but had no idea how to express it. Instead, they made small talk about her brother's job at the Steam Works and about how expensive everything was now.

'Without the orders for my candles that you give me, I'm sure I would have gone under by now,' she said. 'Oh, by the way, I nearly forgot to tell you. Old Nick called and said you should drop by. He's got some information for you.'

'I wish I could spend more time with you, Maggie, but I'd better go and see him right away.' Jake raised his hat, making Maggie giggle once more as she dropped a curtsey and then he strode off towards the foundry, his thoughts full of self-doubt and missed opportunities.

When Jake returned to the hotel, he found that Oliver and Joshua were out, and Billy was sitting at the table trying to remember lists of ingredients for the recipe book he wanted to compile. Jake had just finished telling them the news that Old Nick had given him.

'That's just typical brutish behaviour from my father!' said Charlotte, 'To invent a machine with absolutely no care or consideration for human life. And fancy calling it The Beast!'

'I can't really visualise it,' said Sadie.

'By all accounts, it's like a big waggon,' said Jake, 'Horses would have pulled it if any were alive, but now men must tow it. My guess is that prisoners will haul it to where they will deploy it, and then soldiers will take over in the face of any conflict. Old Nick told me that two massive canisters are mounted on the back and filled with compressed steam. They are giant versions of the one I had made in Bristol for my mono-scoot. Old Nick didn't make them; Fotheringay called him into the factory to strengthen the axles. Anyway, on the front of the waggon are three cannons powered by compressed steam, but each firing something different. The one that poses the least danger to life and limb fires a jet of water so powerful that it will knock a man over; the second cannon shoots a load of steel ball bearings, which will indiscriminately pepper a crowd with shot, while the third delivers a jet of compressed steam and would target an individual, flaying him alive with boiling vapour.'

'Oh! It's just too horrid!' cried Charlotte.

'This ties up with what Edward told us,' said Sadie, 'The planned strike and protest march.'

'Yes, I'm certain of it,' said Jake.

'Isn't it an indictment of my father and the Government that they should use science as a means of oppressing the people, when you are using compressed steam with your skating boardy thing to invent something that could be good for people,' commented Charlotte.

'It's a mono-scoot,' corrected Jake.

'So, is there anything we can do? You are usually fired up to invent something to thwart my father's schemes. Has it stumped you? Is that why you look so glum?'

'No, no. I mean, I have got a few ideas, but that's not it. It's Maggie.'

'What's wrong with Maggie?' asked Charlotte. 'Is she poorly?'

'No, not at all. Actually, it's me, really. Well, me and

Maggie. Mostly me!'

'What do you mean?' asked Sadie, 'For a lad who knows how to fit a dozen cogs together and make something happen, you're not exactly fitting your words together to make any sense.'

'That's just it. I like Maggie more than anyone could imagine. More than Maggie could guess, but I don't know how to express it. I don't know what to say or what to do next.'

'I've never met Maggie, but she sounds a sweet girl,' said Sadie, 'If you are feeling shy, sometimes it's not about words; it can be just looking into her eyes that little bit longer than you are used to, or a gentle touch on her arm.' Then, slipping into her Manchester vernacular, she added, 'Use tha reet hand, mind. Tha' dun't want to be firin' a dart into her!' They all started to laugh. 'Why don't you just kiss her?' continued Sadie, 'There would be no mistaking your feelings, then. If she pulls away, apologise; if she doesn't, then all well and good!'

'But, but. I don't know how. I've never kissed anyone before, and no one has ever kissed me. I don't know how to do it.'

'Oh, come 'ere, tha big ninny,' replied Sadie, and she rose up on her tiptoes and planted her lips on Jake's mouth. After a few seconds, she stopped, 'Open your lips a little, Jake. You can't kiss if your mouth is clamped shut!' That happened naturally for the astonished Jake because he drew a quick breath, and before he could close his mouth again, Sadie resumed her kiss. This time it was a a full minute before she broke away.

'Oh my!' gasped Jake.

'Very good, Jake. Another tip. Don't just stand there; you need to embrace her. Perhaps start with your hand on her waist and then move it around to her back so you can pull her in tight. Watch what you are doing with that metal hand, though! I don't suppose you could fit one covered in velvet for when you feel romantic?' The laughter that followed removed any embarrassment on Jake's part. 'Mind you,' continued Sadie, 'When I was a working girl, I didn't let any of my clients kiss me, but I did have a couple of boyfriends in the past.'

'If it's any consolation, Jake,' said Charlotte, 'I've never been kissed either.'

'What, never?' exclaimed Sadie.

'No, never. I mean, my nanny used to kiss me on the forehead when I was little, but my parents kept me on a tight rein. I've never been kissed like that!'

'Ah, well!' said Sadie, 'In for a penny, in for a pound,' and she turned to Charlotte and kissed her. Jake presumed they were demonstrating for his benefit what he should do with his hands as Sadie's hands travelled around Charlotte's back and Charlotte reciprocated. That was far from the truth, they held each other tightly, and neither wanted to break off. Finally, Sadie pulled away and looked Charlotte full in the eye for a few moments before saying softly, 'And here endeth today's lesson.'

'If yer don't mind,' piped up Billy from the back of the room, 'Can I put off my lesson for around five years? I ain't ready for it yet. All I wanna know is: 'Ow do yer spell paprika?'

CHAPTER THIRTEEN

'Ere,' whispered Norma, one of the clerks at the Steam Works to her junior, Audrey, 'Have you ever seen anyone look so nervous?' They both glanced at Robert Greville, who couldn't stop fidgeting. One moment he sat down, the next, he stood up, shifting from one foot to the other. He kept mopping his brow with a white linen handkerchief.

'There's an important looking general already gone in the office.'

'For your information, he's a Field Marshal, not a general, and he's only the man running the country now they've got rid of all the politicians.'

'He is important then! Oh! Here's someone else. Hello, can I...?'

'I know my way,' said the visitor brusquely, pushing past Audrey and entering Fotheringay's office without knocking.

'Charming!' whispered Audrey. 'It's funny; he looked a bit like Mr Fotheringay.'

'That's because he's his brother, Robert.'

Inside the office, Leonard Fotheringay offered his brother a cigar.

'What's all this about?' asked Robert, 'It's dashed inconvenient. It took me an age to get here. I had to walk from the station. I'm a busy man. I've got a farm to run.'

'You're a busy man?' said Field Marshal Bellings drily, 'I've got a country to run!'

'I don't know why you are here,' snapped Leonard Fotheringay, 'All I know is Robert Greville, our shipping agent, asked to see us all in person. He's outside; maybe you noticed him.' His brother shook his head. Leonard Fotheringay opened the door and called Robert Greville in. 'Well! Explain yourself.'

Within his own world, Robert Greville usually felt all-powerful and acted accordingly. Woe betide any of his subordinates he felt were slacking; they would soon find themselves out on the street looking for new employment. Now, however, faced with the mighty Fotheringay family and the new leader of Parliament, he felt decidedly insignificant.

'Erm...'

'Spit it out!' demanded Bellings.

'Erm... It's the Deception. She's lost.'

'What do you mean lost? Find her!' exclaimed Bellings.

'No one knows where she is. First, she was taken, and then she disappeared.'

'Taken?' yelled Robert Fotheringay. 'Explain yourself.'

'I have only just learned about it. The captain of the Deception and her crew were picked up by another ship travelling back to England. As you can imagine, I was amazed to see him walk into my office yesterday when I had expected him to be on his way to America with his ...special cargo. He told me that he had been forced to hand the ship over to a fierce bunch of pirates who sailed the ship back towards Africa. Maybe she will turn up, but no one has seen the Deception since.'

'Oh, this is bad,' muttered Bellings, 'I presume the insurance will only cover us for the value of the palm oil and the ivory we declared was on the ship, not the human cargo, for which we paid considerably more.'

'A payment we made upfront,' added Robert Fotheringay.

'I'm sorry,' said Greville, 'But it gets worse. The file for the Deception has gone missing. We don't have any documents, and we will need them if we wish to make an insurance claim.'

'You must have misfiled them, man!' roared Bellings.

'No, we have searched the office three times. Anyway, I distinctly remember filing them away in the correct place the day we had those awful visitors.'

'What visitors?' asked Leonard Fotheringay.

'A couple of strumpets came to the office, and made a scene. I've never seen anyone dressed like them in my life! Petticoats and corsets on show....'

Suddenly, there was a knock on the door. Leonard Fotheringay strode over and opened it.

'Yes. What is it?'

'Excuse me, sir,' replied Norma, her voice quivering with fear, 'Sorry to interrupt, but Mr Hastings said you would want to see this. Apparently, it's been circulating on the streets for a few days.' Fotheringay snatched the booklet from her hands and slammed the door in her face.

'Charming!' she muttered under her breath.

'I don't see why this is so dammed important,' complained Leonard Fotheringay. It's just another of those trashy comics that seek to glorify some traitorous criminals.' They all looked at the copy of "The Chronicles of the Rebel Runaways" that Leonard Fotheringay had thrown down on the table.

'Damm it. Doesn't that illustration on the front depict your daughter, my niece Charlotte?' asked Robert Fotheringay.

'I have disowned her, but yes. I fear it is her.' Fotheringay turned over a page to reveal another illustration - a three-masted sailing ship under which was the caption - the Deception.

'It says here the slaves were all returned to Africa,' read Bellings. 'Confound it! Our money is lost.'

'Let me see the cover again,' demanded Greville, 'That's exactly how the strumpets who came to my office were dressed, and more than that, look! There is a drawing of an airship. I haven't told you this yet, but the Deception's captain told me the pirates arrived in an airship.'

'You had better do something about this,' Robert Fotheringay warned his brother. 'And you!' he said to Bellings. 'I don't take too kindly to losing a small fortune on this venture,' and he stormed from the room, slamming the door behind him.

'Where better for us to show off our fashions than Bond Street?' said Sadie.

'I have heard of it but never visited. So why is it so famous?' asked Charlotte.

'I've never been before, either, but I used to have this client, a rather dissolute old chap and a bit of a dandy. He told me that in his youth, this was simply the place to be seen. Men and women, dressed to the nines, would spend their time parading up and down, showing off their finery. They called themselves the Bond Street Loungers. It's not quite the place it was but still, let's show everyone what a Rebel looks like.'

They hadn't got far before Charlotte tripped on an uneven paving stone.

'Oh bother! I've ripped the hem of my petticoat.'

'Let me see. The heel of your boot has snagged it. I'm sure it can be mended. Perhaps take an inch off all the way around.'

'What a nuisance! It's trailing on the ground now.'

'We've come to the right street. There are lots of fashion houses here as well as the swanky shops. Someone should be able to sort it out. Let's try this one, Madame Marguerite.' Charlotte and Sadie climbed the stairs leading to the dressmaker's establishment. It occupied the floor above a shop selling expensive luggage.

'It could do with some redecoration up here,' whispered Charlotte. 'Maybe it's not quite as exclusive as we thought it might be.'

'Never mind. It might not cost us as much.' As they entered through a door off the landing and into a small reception room, a bell rang and a young lady emerged from a room beyond, holding the sleeve of a garment that she was evidently in the middle of sewing. She was of a similar age to Charlotte, with dark tousled hair, olive skin and deep brown eyes. She looked a little surprised to see the visitors.

'Hello,' she said, 'I wasn't expecting anyone. I'm afraid Madame Marguerite has had to go out to meet a client. She shouldn't be long. Please take a seat.'

'I'd love to see what's through there,' said Sadie, nodding towards the room the seamstress had come from. 'We both love sewing.'

'Do you? Well, considering your get-ups, I suppose you would have to. I don't suppose it would do any harm. This first room is the fitting room. We often make a toile first - that's a version of the garment in a cheap fabric, like calico - so we can make adjustments without spoiling the expensive stuff. The client stands on that platform for the fitting. Then through this door is the room where I draft the patterns and do the sewing.'

'So, is it just you, or does Madame Marguerite sew too?'

'Only me. Madame Marguerite is more "front of house". She meets the clients. I'm not usually permitted to see them until a garment has been commissioned. Oh! Here she is now. We had better come out of here.' They hadn't got far before they encountered an elegantly dressed woman in her fifties who swept into the fitting room.

'Jenny, what iz ze meaning of zis? Why are zey in 'ere?'

'Excuse me, Madame Marguerite, it's our fault; we positively demanded that Jenny showed us around,' said Sadie, 'We called to see if you could repair Charlotte's petticoat.' Madame Marguerite looked them up and down, wrinkling her nose as though she had detected a bad smell.

'I don't sink so. You do not 'ave the required 'je ne sais quoi' to be acceptable.' She held open the door to the reception room. 'Jenny, pliz show zem out.' Madame Marguerite closed the door behind them but did not shut it completely. Something was troubling her, so she stayed close behind it and listened.

'I'm sorry,' said Jenny softly. Wait.' Jenny scribbled her address on a scrap of paper, 'Come and see me at my room in Holborn after seven. I can do it. I know who you are!'

'I know who you are,' thought Madame Marguerite. 'Who are they?' What had she half-remembered? Then, it came to her. She had been to the police station recently in connection with a client who owed her money. It was something she had seen then! 'Get on wiz your work,' she hissed to Jenny, 'I 'ave to go out again.' She needed to revisit the police station to confirm her suspicions.

'Do you think it's a trap?' asked Sadie as they walked back to the hotel.

'No, Jenny seemed nice, not like Madame Marguerite, and in any case, if she wanted to trap us, why would she say she knew who we were?'

At that very moment, the aforesaid Madame Marguerite was staring at a crude poster in the police station. Drawings resembling the girls had been cut out of another document and pasted onto it. She wasn't to know that they had been snipped from one of Edward's story books. Below, written in bold letters, were the words "Wanted! Enemies of the Realm."

CHAPTER FOURTEEN

'Here we are,' said Sadie, 'I don't reckon Jenny gets paid a lot if she's living in this area. Mind you, it's ten times better than The Rookery.'

'Her note says she is on the second floor.'

'Come in,' said Jenny a few moments later, 'I'll make a cup of tea.' Sadie and Charlotte surveyed the room. It was neat and clean, but cramped and sparsely furnished. Jenny had drawn a curtain across an alcove, and they could see part of an iron bedstead. A kettle simmered on a small black stove. Charlotte and Sadie walked over to the large casement window, which opened onto a narrow balcony, 'The view is the best thing about this room,' said Jenny, 'That's Lincoln's Inn Fields that you can see there. It's a lovely park. I share the balcony with the family next door. I listen out for the children when the parents are at work at night in the bakery.'

'We've brought the petticoat. Thanks so much for offering to do it for us,' said Charlotte.

'I'm sorry you had to see the sour side of Madame Marguerite. Actually, that's the side I usually see. She can be as sweet as pie to rich visitors. Positively fawning.'

'She has a strange accent,' said Charlotte, 'It sounds like French, but not quite. Is she from one of the French colonies?' Jenny burst out laughing.

'No, far from it. I think she's from Birmingham. She puts on that accent. She doesn't realise everyone laughs at her behind her back. I tell you what else is funny. She thinks Marguerite is a classy name, but it just means a common daisy. What's more, she won't call me by my real name because it's French!'

'What is your real name?' asked Sadie.

'It's Genevieve.'

'Then, from now on, we will call you Genevieve,' said Charlotte. 'Why have you got a French name?'

'Have you heard of the Huguenots?' asked Genevieve. Sadie shook her head, but Charlotte nodded,

'They were the Protestants expelled from Catholic France over a hundred years ago, weren't they?'

'That's right, and through the generations ever since, my family has always made sure the children could speak French, and they gave us Fench names in the hope that one day we would go back to our motherland.'

'You said you knew who we were.' Sadie was looking thoughtful. Genevieve smiled and pointed to a small table on which was piled probably every issue of Edward's Chronicles.

'It's not just the different exploits that you get up to

that I love; it's your sense of style. The work I do for Madame Marguerite is so old-fashioned.'

Suddenly, there was a loud hammering at the door, and a voice rang out:

'Open up in the name of Her Majesty's Government.' The three girls froze. Then touching a finger to her lips, Genevieve grabbed a set of keys from a hook, moved the kettle off the hob, and gestured for Charlotte and Sadie to follow her to the window. Once all three were on the balcony, she shut the window behind her and opened her neighbours' window, which had been left ajar.

'This is how I listen out for the children,' she whispered. 'I'll lock it from the inside.' They tiptoed through the room, thankful that the two children snuggled up on the bed were asleep, then they waited and listened at the door, flinching when they heard the crash as Genevieve's door was broken down by the policemen. After a few moments, they heard a voice:

'Looks like we missed them this time. I reckon they was here, though 'cause there's three empty tea cups and the kettle is still hot.'

'I told you it would take longer to walk here than you said!'

'Bleeding horse flu!'

'How? How...?' whispered Charlotte to Genevieve after they had heard footsteps heading for the stairs.

'There is only one other person who knows where I live, and that's Madame Marguerite. It has to be her. I will never go back to work for her, even if I starve.'

'I'm very sorry, it's worse than that, for it's not a matter of choice. You can't go back. In the eyes of the law, we are enemies of the state and those policemen will know you have helped us. If you went back, they could arrest you for treason,' said Charlotte.

'I bet you that Madame Marguerite sacrificed you in the hope of collecting a large reward,' declared Sadie.

'Check the coast is clear and grab whatever you need or want from your room,' said Charlotte, 'Is there a back way out of here in case they have left someone guarding the door?'

Genevieve nodded. 'Better than that,' she said, 'There's a tunnel that starts in the basement and comes out at the edge of Lincoln's Inn Fields.'

'You must come with us back to our hotel,' said Sadie, 'Welcome to the Rebel Runaways.'

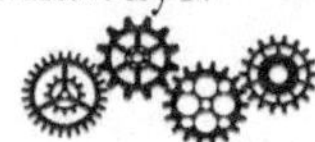

'You've been very quiet lately, Charlotte,' said Sadie.

'I know, I've been thinking.' Everyone was back at the hotel now, although Oliver was still in his room. Jake was hard at work making clockwork Spiders: this time to a modified design. Genevieve, having been introduced to the rest of the crew, was dazed by the speed of recent events. It seemed that one minute, she was reading about the exploits of the Rebel Runaways and the next she was one of them. There was a knock at the door, Joshua opened it to reveal young Tom, a copy of the evening newspaper in his hand.

'Mr Moon asked for this,' he said.

'Don't worry, I'll take it to him. I want to ask him something anyway,' said Charlotte.

'Isn't he sweet?' said Genevieve after Tom had gone, 'He fetched up a trundle bed and wouldn't let me help him make it up.'

'Yes,' agreed Sadie. 'We can depend on Tom. If anyone comes looking for us at the front desk, we can guarantee he will send them packing saying he hasn't seen us.'

'I'm finding it hard to believe I'm wanted by the law,' said Genevieve. 'I suppose this is what my ancestors faced when they were thrown out of France. An uncertain future!'

'You've been a long time,' said Sadie as Charlotte returned to the room, 'Don't tell me - his eyesight was so blurry after all the wine he poured down his neck yesterday that you had to read the newspaper to him!'

'No,' laughed Charlotte, 'In fact, he was surprisingly lucid. Sit down. Having talked to Oliver, I've something to discuss that involves you, Sadie - and you too Genevieve.'

'Goodness,' said Genevieve, 'Oliver's the one person I haven't met yet. What's he like?'

'He's a gentleman, and a protector, and he's very charming,' explained Sadie, 'Unless he's drunk, which he is a lot of the time, in which case he can be unpredictable, unreliable and prone to getting into fights. But he is never aggressive with us. We support each other.'

'I don't want to push you two into anything against your will,' said Charlotte. 'Sadie, firstly, can you describe Foula to Genevieve?'

'Well, let me see. It's pretty much as far away as you can get from here and still be in Britain, so we feel quite safe there. We get on well with the locals; the Laird is Oliver's brother.'

'Is it pretty?' asked Genevieve.

'I suppose so, in a bleak, desolate, craggy kind of way. There aren't really many trees or people. Just moorlands and seabirds. And wind; it's always windy.'

'Tell her how you feel when you are there,' prompted Charlotte.

'Well, I feel safe and it's good to have a rest, but...' Her voice tailed off.

'Admit it. You get bored, don't you?'

Sadie nodded. 'I enjoy it when we are altering clothes, especially when I'm using your sewing machine.'

'You've got a sewing machine?' exclaimed Genevieve in surprise. 'Madame Marguerite refused to get one. She said they were too expensive.'

'Yes, I have. Actually, that brings me to you, Genevieve. Tell me about your job as a seamstress.'

'If you take my relationship with Madame Marguerite out of the picture, I just loved it, especially when I had the opportunity to be creative, which rarely happened.'

'And, changing the subject, you said your parents taught French to you in case the opportunity arose to return to France,' continued Charlotte.

'Yes, that's right. I'd love to go there. I've never been.'

'Where's all this leading?' asked Sadie.

'I'll tell you where it's leading,' chuckled Charlotte, 'It's leading us to Paris.'

'Paris?' echoed Sadie and Genevieve.

'Now, I'll tell you what we are going to do. I asked Oliver if he would lend us some money. He would have given it to us, but I insisted we had to be businesslike. We are going to set up our own fashion house in Paris, and you, Genevieve, will run it. Sadie and I will design for it and you can too - and we will introduce our own unique style to the world. Where Paris leads, London and New York will follow.'

'I can't believe it! Yes, yes, yes!' enthused Genevieve. 'I have a suggestion for a name. We could call the house "Belle Rebelle". It means Beautiful Rebel.'

Joshua had been following the conversation with interest. 'If we are going to spend more time in France, perhaps you could teach me a few words of French. There are many of my African brothers there, from colonies like Senegal and Mali. It would be good to be able to converse with them and share their food and music.'

'Food!' piped up Billy. 'Now, you're talking! Ain't the French supposed to be good cooks? I'm not eating any snails and frogs' legs, mind!'

'I have another idea,' said Genevieve, 'I am sure the French would love to read Edward's Chronicles, especially as they poke fun at the British Government. I could translate them. It would help create a demand for Belle Rebelle. Soon, young girls all over France will want to look like you. I know I can't wait to transform myself. Now I know how the caterpillar feels when it becomes a butterfly!'

When Edward thought about his wife, Arabella, especially when he was away from home, he was confident that he loved her. It was just that it was harder to come to that conclusion when he was in her company.

'More tea, dear?' Edward nodded without much enthusiasm.

It's not just that life at home is rather tame,' he thought, *'After all, one can't expect to spend one's whole life flying around in an airship having adventures. It's just that I struggle to find common ground. I know I can't breathe a word of my life with the Rebel Runaways to her. She wouldn't understand, and the first thing she would do is to tell her father, and then he would tell the authorities, and who knows what chaos would ensue?'*

'Have I told you that I saw a darling little hat...'

I don't know what Arabella would make of the clothes that Charlotte and Sadie wear. I must say, at first, I was a little shocked myself. I suppose I had quite a sheltered upbringing and was told to blend in and not stand out, but now I feel proud to be in their company. To walk along a street knowing that heads are turning gives me a sense of belonging.'

'Are you listening, Edward?'

'Yes, dear. Have you heard the news that the trades unions are...'

'Oh! Boring, boring politics again. How many times must I say it? I'm just not interested. Let them squabble amongst themselves. Don't include me!'

That's part of the problem,' he thought, *'She doesn't realise that politics affects everyone, and, unlike the Rebels, she certainly has no interest in the welfare of the working man. I want to be tender towards her, but she doesn't make it easy.'* Edward smiled at his wife.

'That's a funny expression on your face,' she remarked.

'I just wondered if we might have an early night,' he said.

'I hope you are not getting any ideas; it's not our night!'

'No, no,' he replied, trying to mask his disappointment, 'I'm just feeling rather tired.'

'It's all that gallivanting you have to do with that stupid job. I don't know why you won't accept a nice easy job in Daddy's bank!'

'But my work for Reuters is important. I seek out the truth.'

'Money is important. The banks provide stability.'

We look at the world from completely different viewpoints,' thought Edward miserably, *There are two aspects of my life I feel completely at ease with. One is my work as a reporter for Reuters. I especially like the fact that we are using modern methods like the telegram service to relay the news far and wide. The other is my work as the author of The Chronicles. I get tremendous pleasure in writing stories that are enjoyed by so many. But as far as understanding my wife goes, I'm all at sea. Is there a soft centre inside that hard shell? In fact, what does she look like, anyway? I've never seen her without her clothes on. She always gets changed into her nightgown in her dressing room, and when we do, you know, the deed, she insists the curtains are drawn, and the lights are off. I don't suppose Sadie...'*

'Edward! You are daydreaming again!'

'Sorry, dear.'

I must stop myself thinking of Charlotte and Sadie in that way. And now there's Genevieve too. I'm very excited at the thought of her translating my books into French. She's another beauty too with her dark, smouldering eyes and..'

'Edward!'

CHAPTER FIFTEEN

Since discovering an interest in food and cooking, Billy had developed a good relationship with several London restaurants. He had dined at them all, courtesy of Oliver, but his passion lay in knowing what happened behind the scenes, in the kitchen.

'I can't quite figure out where I fit in,' he thought as he entered Mario's Chophouse. *'Collectin' recipes is a start, I s'pose. I'm interested, but would anyone else be bovvered? I've 'ad a butcher's at that Mrs Beeton's book which lots of people 'ave talked abaht. Yeah, it's got recipes but also lots of advice abaht ow to manage yer servants and the like. It ain't exactly written fer the likes of me. Then again,'* he thought as he adjusted his top hat, smoothed down his brightly-coloured, embroidered waistcoat and adjusted his silk neckerchief, *'Maybe there ain't many people like*

me!'

'Billy, il mio piccolo amico,' greeted a waiter. Billy had been here often enough to know that he was being called a little friend, and that was exactly how he felt. He was amongst friends and felt more of an affinity with the staff than with the diners.

'Are you eating today because, looking at your clothes, I must warn you, we don't have rainbow trout on the menu!'

'Ha ha! Cheek! Actually, I have just come in for a natter with Mario.'

A few minutes earlier, in the coffee house opposite, Billy's arrival at Mario's had been observed by none other than his arch-enemy, Hastings. The fact that Billy was openly strutting around London was particularly galling to him because Billy had somehow evaded capture twice before; once when Grimes had apprehended him before the debacle of the big cannon explosion and once when he had been a few minutes away from being hanged at Newgate. Now, Hastings needed to pay for his coffee and pursue Billy, but he couldn't catch the eye of the waitress.

'Dammit! Will someone attend to me!' he shouted, causing every head to turn in his direction. He knew the coffee cost one penny, but the smallest coin he had was a threepenny bit. He could have left it on the table, so the waitress would have a tip, but that was not in his nature. Eventually, his bill paid, he burst into Mario's, casting around wildly for Billy.

'Sir, please wait to be seated,' called a waiter, ignored by Hastings.

At that moment, Billy was leaving the kitchen via the back door. Mario had been too busy to talk to him, so he intended to return later. At the end of the alleyway that led back to the street, Billy had to step over a young urchin lying on the cobbles. The boy raised his head weakly.

'Give us a bob, guvnor. I ain't eaten for donkey's.'

'Sorry, mate. Ain't got a ha'penny to spare. All I got is a coin for the street gang's toll. But I can nip in and scrounge yer some grub if yer fancy it."

If Hastings had been born an animal, he would have been a bull; a belligerent beast, with wild, red eyes, snorting and slobbering and charging around, leaving a trail of chaos. A more intelligent creature would have noticed two doors connecting the restaurant to the kitchens, one through which the waiters brought the food and another through which they returned. Hastings was not such a creature and, having realised that Billy was not dining, he shouldered through the nearest door and collided with a waiter bearing a tray of food. It was an unfortunate encounter. The tray flew through the air, the plate clattered to the floor and the gravy boat deposited its contents down the front of Hastings' suit.

'Where is he!' roared Hastings. As he shoved the stunned waiter aside he felt a hand grasp him around the throat and he was propelled backwards and pinned against the wall. A large, angry chef was pointing a sharp-looking knife at his face.

'I don't know who you look for. I don't care about anyone else. I just care that you are in my kitchen,' snarled Mario. 'That was the last serving for a large table, and now I 'ave to cook it again, so one person will have to wait while everyone else eats. How do you think that affects my reputation?' Mario lowered the knife, hooked it through Hastings' belt and, in one easy movement, sliced right through it. 'I tell you, one delicacy I sometimes cook is Lamb Fries,' said Mario, probing with his knife. 'Do you know what it is made of?'

'No, no,' stammered Hastings, utterly powerless. Mario sliced down Hastings' trousers. Fly buttons pinged in all directions. As his trousers started to descend, Mario's knife probed a little more.

'Testicles! It is made from testicles. I was tempted to try a new dish using yours, but they are such pathetic specimens that it won't be worth my time. Get out of my kitchen!' Mario shoved Hastings towards the back door, where he sprawled on the floor with his trousers around his ankles. He scrambled to his feet, clutching his ruined trousers at the waist, and left the kitchen as quickly as he could. 'You had better wash this knife,' Mario called to the pot boy, who was doubled up with laughter, 'It has been somewhere disgusting!'

Just then, Billy breezed back into the kitchen.

'Hello again!' he said, 'I was just wonderin', any leftovers yer don't want? Cor blimey, wot's all this on the floor? You can't serve that, can yer? Can I 'ave it, an' this plate an all? It's got a bleedin' big chip out of it. You 'ave to sling it anyway. Cheers, mate!'

A few minutes later, as he watched the young urchin devour a portion of grilled lamb chops from a broken plate, an idea started to form in Billy's head.

'I didn't realise I had slept for so long,' said Oliver to Joshua, who appeared to be the only one of the Runaways left in the hotel, 'Think I will stretch my legs,' and with that, Oliver bounded down the stairs and out onto the street.

'Which way?' he thought to himself. *'I know; I'll head to Chelsea. Let's see what the crème de la crème are up to. It's a nice evening. Pity about this damned headache. Well, there's one sure way*

to cure it. Hair of the dog! The Crown; that's as good a pub as any. Just for one, mind. In fact, it's my patriotic duty to toast our Queen.'

It was a typical, modern, city pub, with walls painted dark brown above embossed green tiles. Oliver stepped in a sprightly fashion over a square of mosaic tiles in the vestibule; the rest of the pub's flooring was of bare boards, their varnish worn away in parts, covered with a layer of sawdust to soak up spills.

'Barman, a pint of your finest, please!

I wonder how the Queen is getting on during these strange times. By all accounts, Prince Albert has been ill for quite a while. Tummy troubles! Me, I've a cast-iron stomach! I can eat or drink anything. In fact, that beer seemed to go down without touching the sides. Another, I think.'

The second drink went down as easily as the first. Oliver congratulated himself on his self-discipline as he resisted ordering a third and found himself back outside. He headed for Chelsea.

'See! The headache's gone. S'miracle! I must remember, I'm a wanted man. I keep getting this feeling that I'm being followed. Oh, I don't seem to have my sword stick. Never mind! Just let them try. I'll take them with my bare hands! Now that sounds like a lively pub. I can hear music, Irish music. Always gets the blood coursing around my veins.' From the shadows, Oliver's jovial entrance into the Shamrock was observed. It was part skip, part kick, and the occasional stumble as he attempted to emulate an Irish jig. An hour later, the same eyes watched him totter out onto the street, still dancing, wearing a broad smile and fortified by three pints of Guinness.

'S'good stuff that stout. S'almost like having a meal. Good crowd in there. I love 'em all. Friends for life. Should have learned their names. Probably all called Patrick. Did I have a hat on? Haven't got one now. Never mind. Chelsea beckons.'

Oliver's pursuer was surprised by how briskly his quarry was walking. Of course, he didn't realise that Oliver was on a mission to reach Chelsea, which was a fair way from the hotel. Without a second glance at the numerous pubs that they passed, Oliver skirted around St James's Park, through Belgravia and along the King's Road.

'Here they are,' thought Oliver, *'Cremorne Gardens. The best Pleasure Gardens in London. I'll just buy myself a ticket, and then I'll have myself some pleasure!'*

As Oliver joined the throng in the park, a young woman with an ample cleavage on show whispered in his ear.

'Madam,' he replied, 'I know this is a pleasure garden, but it's a little early in the evening for the particular activity you suggest. Let me buy you a drink. I'm in the mood for dancing just now; then perhaps I shall take up your offer later. You are a pretty little girl!' The prostitute linked her arm with Oliver's, and they headed for a booth where Oliver purchased glasses of wine for them both. Nearby was the tall pagoda-shaped bandstand, surrounded by a raised platform on which at least a hundred people were already dancing and cavorting.

'Madam, our drinks are finished. Would you allow me to escort you to the dance floor?' The young lady, who was named Violet, had no intention of relinquishing her catch. Before the night was out, she intended to lead him to a darker region of the park, where she could do what needed to be done without being disturbed.

Meanwhile, Oliver's shadow was having a little difficulty in finding the shilling needed to purchase the entrance ticket. After a frantic search through his pockets he he handed over a pile of pennies and halfpennies, but by the time he was inside the pleasure garden, his man was nowhere to be seen. Oliver, having acquired two more glasses of wine, was still dancing.

'S'making me dizzy, this Viennese waltz, round and round and round and...Hey! You watch where you are going, you clumsy oaf!...Yes, I'm talking to you. You bashed my dear sweet Violet. The prettiest flower in the park...I don't like your tone... That's not a nice way to refer to my dancing partner...So you think you are tougher than me, do you? I may have had a few, but I could take you with one hand behind my back. Come on, then. Over there where it is dark.'

Oliver ignored Violet's protestations and the two men strode towards the fringes of the park. Oliver hung his jacket on a bush, held up his fists and waited for his opponent to make his move. Oliver expected to defend himself against a rushed onslaught with fists flying, but instead, the man mirrored Oliver's own stance, and the two circled each other warily. Oliver parried a left jab , returning a left hook which missed its target. Then came another left; this time it connected and Oliver's head jerked back, but he was only momentarily stunned and closed in to land a punch to his opponent's stomach, followed by a swift right hook that glanced off the man's chin. The two men were eyeball to eyeball, trading punches. By now, a small crowd of onlookers had gathered, the most vociferous among them being young Violet, who saw her evening's earnings in danger of slipping away. Finally, after yet another punch to the solar plexus, Oliver's adversary slowly dropped to his knees.

'I'm done,' he uttered. The crowd fully expected Oliver to finish him off with a swinging punch, but instead, he reached out a hand to pull him to his feet.

'Very well fought, Sir. It could easily have gone the

other way.'

'But what about me?' squealed Violet.

'Oh! I am sorry, my dear. All the passion has been beaten out of me. Let me give you something to ease your disappointment.' Oliver reached into his pocket and pulled out a gold sovereign. The crowd laughed as he said, 'You truly have missed out. I make love with as much energy as I fight. It would have been a night to remember!' As Violet slipped away, she thought:

'I'll certainly remember this night. I've earned a lot more money than I would 'ave for a quick tumble behind the rose bushes, plus he bought me a few wines. A good night all round! I can go 'ome now and see 'ow my babbies are.' She looked over her shoulder to see the former adversaries arm in arm as they staggered over to a booth to buy food and wine.

'My name is Peter. I tell you, if I hadn't been digging all day, it would have been a different outcome. It fair sapped my strength.'

'So what were you digging? Potatoes?'

'No, I've been preparing a field to be the base for the Air-Fleet. You know, balloons and airships and the like. It's the third and last one I've done. I got paid today.'

'Tell me, Peter. Where are these fields? Another wine?'

'Well, it's supposed to be a secret, but I can't see the harm in telling you.'

The fun and games in Cremorne Gardens continued into the night but one man was oblivious to it all, even to the daredevil artiste who crossed the Thames on a high wire and descended in the Park amid hooting and cheering. Oliver lay on his back on the grass, dead to the world and snoring loudly.

'Oliver! Oliver! I think it's time we headed back to the

hotel. We can get a boat up the Thames to cut down on the walk.' Oliver opened his eyes and smiled.

'Hello, Joshua.' Joshua was holding Oliver's sword stick, which he had retrieved from the Crown, his top hat which was on the bar in the Shamrock and his jacket, which had been draped over a bush in the Pleasure Gardens.

'That was a fun night. Ow!' Oliver felt his bruised chin, 'How did that happen?'

'If I tell you now, you'll probably forget by the morning,' laughed Joshua, hauling Oliver to his feet.

'Actually, I have remembered something important. I'll tell you. I know where the three fields that the Air-Fleet have relocated to are.'

'So it wasn't just pleasure tonight, it was business too.'

Oliver wagged a finger:

'Always pleasure first, my dear boy!'

CHAPTER SIXTEEN

'I know there is an idea in there,' said Billy to Charlotte, hitting himself on the head. 'But I ain't so good as you and Jake at making plans. I don't know how to get it going.'

'What's the basis of your idea?' prompted Charlotte.

'Soup.'

'You want to sell soup?'

'Nah, I wanna give it away.'

'Sounds more like a charity than a business.'

'Yeah, that's right. Fings were 'ard enough before all this 'orse flu business, finkin' back to the times before I met you lot. Now, for kids livin' on the street, it's a million times worse.'

'So, do you intend to spend all your time making

soup?'

'I don't mind chippin' in, but we ain't in one place all the bleedin' time. I ain't plannin' to leave the Rebels. When we're on our travels, I wanna carry on cookin' for all you lot!".'

'I must say, your cooking's getting better,' said Jake, joining them, 'When I think back to your early rock cakes, it's a wonder any of us have any teeth left!'

'Bloomin' cheek!'

'So, what you want to do is set up something that will run in your absence,' continued Charlotte. Billy nodded. 'Actually, A lady called Mrs Blenkinsop-Smythe told me that providing free soup used to be illegal. The Government wanted to force destitute people into the workhouses, but parliament amended the law after the Irish Potato Famine. Mrs Blenkinsop-Smythe used to visit our house, trying - unsuccessfully - to get my father's business to donate to her charity. I'm sure I could trace her. She lives in Mayfair.'

'Are you thinking of setting up a restaurant then?' asked Jake.

'Nah! I ain't got a clue 'ow it'd work, but I would rather we gave out soup in places where people live,' replied Billy.

'It might sound a little harsh, but I reckon some restaurants would be very pleased that street urchins were being fed in their own districts rather than begging outside the restaurant doors,' said Charlotte.

'Forgive me for asking, but how do you actually make soup?' asked Jake.

'Easy Peasy! Get a load o' scraps o' vegetables and bits of meat and boil 'em up until everyfink is cooked,' replied Billy, confidently.

'The boiling is going to be important because otherwise you'll poison everyone; our water is so impure,' said Charlotte.

'Excuse me a moment; I've got an idea. I'll just go and sketch it,' said Jake.

'So, you need some volunteers,' said Sadie, joining in with the conversation, 'And maybe Charlotte's Lady Doo-Dah would help find some, but I would have thought they would be more likely to contribute their time if there was some financial backing behind it.'

'I don't wanna ask fer a handout from Oliver, even though he's rich,' said Billy.

'Quite right,' agreed Sadie. 'I'm sure Oliver wouldn't mind giving the enterprise a little boost just to get it all going, but the bloke I had in mind is Edward, or rather The Chronicles. He sells a lot of stories now, and he might agree to give you a regular donation. He could even publish a list of where to find the soup stations.'

'I'm sure he would,' said Jake, 'Look at this!' They gathered around Jake's drawing. 'It's made from oil drums. Remember those drums of palm oil on the Deception?'

'Yes, that African village was pleased to get those,' said Billy.

'See, there's half a drum at the bottom. You light a fire in there. It's welded to a full one on top. That's where you cook the soup,' continued Jake.

Charlotte pointed to the drawing:

'Trust you to include some cogs. What's that on top?'

'That, my dear girl, is a lid incorporating a clockwork stirrer. Not only that, once the cooking begins, the lid will seal itself for a prescribed time, say an hour or two, so no one can get at the soup until it's ready.'

'That's fantastic,' said Billy. 'Then the drums can be

outside. No need for premises.'

'Hopefully, charity workers could collect unwanted food from restaurants,' said Charlotte. 'Maybe the drums could be outside churches if we can persuade the clergy to help.'

'If we can scrounge the drums from somewhere, I'm certain Old Nick will do all the metalwork,' added Jake, 'And if I add a tall chimney, it will not only take the smoke away, but it will also look like a railway engine.'

'Perfect for a soup station,' said Billy with a gratified smile.

Jake was in the hotel room polishing his new invention.

'Is your boardy-scoot finished?' asked Charlotte

'It's called a mono-scoot,' replied Jake patiently, 'And yes, it's finished. I just need to fill up the compressed steam chamber.'

'Oh, look at that?' exclaimed Sadie, entering the room, 'Your scooty-board. It looks wonderful.'

'I fought it was called a scooty-deck 'cause it's usin' the deck from the Deception,' piped up Billy.

'For heaven's sake. It's called a mono-scoot!'

If you ask me,' said Oliver, who had just walked into the room, 'I'd call it a death trap!'

'If you were riding it, it most likely would be!' teased Sadie. 'It's teetotal only!'

'How dare you utter that foul swear word in my company!' replied Oliver, joining in with the laughter.

Who fancies a trip to Regent's Park to top up the steam canisters?' asked Jake.

'I'll come,' said Joshua. He had been trying to make

sense of a list of French irregular verbs that Charlotte had prepared for him and needed a distraction. 'I'm looking forward to seeing your skatey-scoot in action.' Jake rolled his eyes in despair.

The last of the evening sun glistened on the ornamental gates leading into Regent's Park, casting long shadows behind Jake, Joshua and Sadie.

'I'm glad I don't have to wear one of them on my back,' said Sadie, pointing to the metal canisters that Jake and Joshua were wearing, 'They look reet heavy.'

'They're not light,' agreed Jake, 'On account of them having triple walls to withstand the pressure of the steam. As far as I remember, the steam pipe leading to Buckingham Palace runs just beyond those trees, so we are close to where they created a junction when they tested the Tiberius cannon. Ah! Shhh! I spy an armed guard.'

'What shall we do?'

'I could knock him out,' said Joshua, 'One blow should do it; he's a puny little fellow.'

'I can kill him with a dart. I've brought the Glove,' said Sadie.

'No, no,' replied Jake. 'Two reasons; firstly, it's not his fault he's been put on duty here. He's only a young lad; unless he tries to harm us, we should let him be. Secondly, I don't want to alert anyone to the fact that we have been here. I may need to come back and fill up the canisters again.'

'I think I need to use my feminine charms, then.'

'Hmm, you may be right. I'm wearing my toolkit hand, so I will only need five minutes to undo the valve and fill up the canisters. But we do need to get him away from here.

I have a plan.'

Five minutes later, they were ready. Cedric, the young guard, was at his post and extremely bored. He felt that he had drawn the short straw with this assignment. It wouldn't be too bad if he had someone to talk to, but the army was short-staffed, with extra reserves needed to patrol unruly parts of the city. He yawned: nothing ever happened to break the monotony. Then suddenly, he was startled by a woman's scream. He grasped his musket and aimed in the direction of the noise. Just as another scream rang out, he jumped in fright as a large man sprinted past him through the shadows from a different direction. It happened so quickly that Cedric missed his chance to fire at the man, but he wasn't inclined to follow him now because the woman had started to wail.

'Help me. For the love of God, help me!' sobbed Sadie.

Cedric felt duty bound to investigate. The woman was clearly distressed; besides, he couldn't listen to that noise all night! He shouldered his musket and crept gingerly towards the crying lady. As soon as Cedric was out of sight, Jake, carrying both canisters, moved swiftly to the steam junction point and began the process of extracting the high-pressure steam. Meanwhile, Joshua had doubled back and was hiding behind a bush, keeping watch over Sadie, who was lying on the ground with her hands tied together.

'Hello,' called Cedric nervously.

'Oh, thank God you have come to save me.'

'What happened?'

'It was that brute; he tied me up. I don't know what he was going to do to me, but something spooked him and he ran away.' Joshua smiled as he watched the soldier spin round, worried that the 'brute' might return.

'Please, can you untie me?'

'Oh, yes. Sorry,' stammered Cedric, and placing his musket on the ground, he began loosening the knots that bound Sadie. He turned out to be rather fast at undoing knots so, in an attempt to keep him occupied longer, Sadie struggled to get to her feet then fell back with an anguished cry, her petticoats flailing all around her.

'What is it?'

It's my ankle. I think I've twisted it. Please can you rub it?'

'Me? Oh, what? Oh, dear! I don't think I...Oh my!'

'Please,' implored Sadie, 'Please,' Cedric slowly stretched out a hand, 'It won't bite,' said Sadie. Gently, the bashful soldier started to rub Sadie's ankle. 'Oh, that's feeling better already.' Cedric was concentrating so hard on this unexpected duty that he failed to hear a bird call in the distance. Sadie and Joshua noticed it, however. It sounded like a Skua, one of the giant seabirds from Foula, and they both knew that it was the signal that Jake had finished.

'Please help me to my feet. I think I can walk now. Can you escort me to the gate?'

'I'm sorry; I ought to return to my post.'

'Never mind, I'll manage. You won't tell anyone about this, will you? I wouldn't like my reputation besmirched.'

'Err, no, of course not.'

'You are sweet. Perhaps I could see you again one night when you are off duty to say thank you.'

Cedric watched the mysterious lady limp down the path to the park gates. 'It must be a trick of the fading light,' he thought, because it looked like she was walking normally just before she disappeared from sight.

'Show us how your scooty-skate works, Jake,' said Sadie.

'I'll be glad to,' replied Jake, not rising to the bait. He wasn't sure if the crew were deliberately teasing him or not. 'The steam canister is hidden under the deck. I know we took two to the park, but the other is a spare. It has a clockwork motor that runs at three speeds, so if I stand on it, see, because it's got two wheels at the back and one at the front, it's quite stable, then if I release this lever, it moves.' With the mono-scoot set to its slowest speed, Jake steered gently around the room. 'It's got a brake too. Now, ingenious invention number one: no need to carry a key because I can wind it by turning the handlebars. Then, we have ingenious invention number two: If I press the boost button, it injects a burst of steam-driven power, so not only will my speed increase, but it will also engage a cog that will rewind the clockwork mechanism. Voilà!' Jake pressed the boost, and the machine shot forward at an alarming speed, directly towards the open window. He pulled hard on the brake, causing his mono-scoot to stop dead. Jake, however, continued forwards, somersaulting over the handlebars and landing in a heap just in front of the window.

'Remind me what "voilà" means, Charlotte,' said Joshua, who had been trying to learn French all morning. 'Does it mean, "What an idiot I look"?'

CHAPTER SEVENTEEN

The following day, after a few adjustments, Jake was ready to try out the mono-scoot. He knew exactly where he wanted to go and who he wanted to see, but felt he needed an excuse to justify his actions.

'I'm going to test the mono-scoot,' he said to the girls, who were busy altering petticoats to fit Genevieve. 'I'll see how it performs transporting loads, and I think an ideal test would be to pick up a box of candles from Maggie. Maybe, I'll even design a trailer to fit it one day, so I could transport several boxes at a time.' The girls exchanged knowing glances and once Jake was out of the room and out of earshot, they fell into fits of giggles.

It worked like a dream, and in no time, Jake was scooting through the alleys and passageways of The

Rookery. Once, spying members of the Black Feathers gang ahead who were waiting to extract toll money from passers-by, he made a sharp turn to avoid them, following a route that was considerably longer but now took no more effort. He would rather his pennies were in his own pocket than in theirs!

'Goodness!' gasped Maggie when she saw Jake glide into her back yard. 'You never cease to amaze me,'

'I think it will be the transport of the future.'

'Fancy being able to think of the future! I find it hard enough to have enough time to deal with the here and now.'

'Are you on your own? Is your brother still working at the Steam Works?'

'Yes, Freddie's on the early shift this week and my mum's gone to deliver some candles round the pubs.'

'How's Freddie getting on?'

Maggie shrugged: 'It's a means to an end. The work's not something he enjoys, but it brings in a few bob. He was talking about that man you told me about. The one who has been trying to find you.'

'Hastings?'

'Yes, that's him. Freddie told me that Hastings had visited every department in the Steam Works and warned them that if any of them dared join tomorrow's General Strike, they would have a very close encounter with his cosh.'

'Don't tell me,' replied Jake, 'After which they would be deemed unfit for work and promptly sacked.' Maggie nodded, 'I remember similar threats when I worked there,' continued Jake, frowning. So Hastings was still on the warpath.

'Actually,' said Maggie, 'Speaking of people trying to

find you, my mum told me there are a lot more soldiers on the streets than normal. She said they were knocking on doors and searching houses.'

'It will be connected with the protest marches tomorrow. After the last incident with that super-cannon, Tiberius, they will be concerned that we might get involved.'

'And will you?'

'You bet your life we will. All the Rebel Runaways will be there.'

'Oh, Jake. I get so worried about you, I...' Maggie was interrupted by someone banging on the front door. It was so loud that they could hear it from the back yard.

'Someone's keen to see you!' remarked Jake.

'Just wait here; I'll look before I open the door. I'm worried.' Maggie stepped through the open door to the kitchen but immediately reappeared. 'Soldiers!' she gasped, 'I can see their red uniforms through the window.'

The gate to the yard was still open. Jake peeped out, then withdrew his head quickly. At each end of the alleyway was a group of soldiers. There was to be no escape that way. Slowly and quietly, Jake closed the yard gate.

'The alleyway is full of soldiers,' he whispered. The visitors at the front door continued to pound on it.

'Hide in there! I'll have to answer the door.' Maggie pointed to the brick outhouse where she kept the supplies for her candle-making business. The door was open, and Jake could see sacks and boxes piled up haphazardly. 'I'll padlock you in.'

A moment later, Maggie opened the door to three disgruntled-looking soldiers.

'You took your time!'

'I'm sorry. I heard you, but I was making candles and

had to turn everything off.' It wasn't an out-and-out lie because she had been making candles, only she had stopped when Jake arrived.

'We've orders to search the place.'

'That's alright. You are welcome. Can I get you boys anything? A cup of tea or a small beer, perhaps?' Maggie had decided that if she tried to get rid of them quickly, they might become suspicious, so instead, she was doing the opposite.

'A small beer would go down nicely.'

'I'll make a cup of tea for myself,' said Maggie. The four of them sat around the kitchen table.

'So you make candles, do you?'

'Yes, mostly I make them out in the yard or in the kitchen if it's raining.'

'We'll be checking the yard after we have finished these beers. Much obliged to you. People around here aren't usually so friendly.'

'I'm glad to help. What are you boys looking for?'

'It's not what. It's who! We're looking for them Rebel Runaways. Personally, I don't know if they exist or are just something made up in storybooks, but orders is orders, so we've got to look for 'em.'

'Next week, they'll have us looking for fairies at the bottom of the garden,' joked one of the others, and they all laughed, including Maggie, who was beginning to think they were good company.

'I mean, this is all very pleasant,' said the third soldier, 'But it ain't exactly why I joined the army.'

'Might be different tomorrer. Should be able to crack a few heads open during this protest march,' replied the first soldier.

'I'm going to polish my bayonet so it slides in good

and proper,'

'Maybe a bit of candlewax will do the trick; we've come to the right place!'

Maggie's blood ran cold, and she rapidly revised her opinion of them. She didn't want them in her house any longer. The first soldier pushed his chair back and stood up:

'Come on, lads. We'd better give this place the once-over.' Maggie followed the men as they made a not-very-thorough search of the house. She was so nervous that her teeth were chattering as she led them out to the yard. Evidence of her profession was all around. One of the soldiers nodded towards the rows of candles hanging on racks.

'Them's a bit skinny,' he laughed.

'That's because I haven't finished dipping them in the beeswax,' explained Maggie, pointing to a metal vat full of molten wax. 'That's what I was seeing to when you were trying to beat my door down.'

'Phwoar!' that stinks. What's in that?' said the second soldier pointing to another vat.

'I'm rendering down animal fat that I get from the butchers to make tallow candles. They're cheaper than the beeswax ones and what most people buy around here. Anyway, have you seen enough now? I need to light the fire under my wax and get back to work.'

'What's in here, then?' asked the third soldier, pointing to the outhouse.

'it's just a storage place. I don't keep the animal fat in it, though, because the rats will have it.' Out of the corner of her eye Maggie saw one of the soldiers shudder at the mention of rats. You couldn't afford to be frightened of rats living in The Rookery. They were everywhere.

'We have to look anyway. It's padlocked. Where's the

key?'

'I keep it in the kitchen.'

The soldiers were discussing rats when Maggie returned with the key. Reluctantly she opened the door, envisioning ending her life on the gallows, hanging side-by-side with Jake, a sign saying 'traitor' hung around her neck.

'Ugh!' One of the soldiers jumped back in fright. Another smashed the butt of his rifle on the rat lying on the floor; a rat that was already dead. Maggie clamped a hand over her mouth. It wasn't the sight of the rat that had made her gasp, but the fact that not only was Jake nowhere to be seen, but her higgledy-piggidly outbuilding now had an orderly pile of boxes stacked against the wall.

The soldiers had recovered their composure.

'Come on, let's get out of here. Roll on tomorrow when we can stamp on strikers instead of rats.'

'Is there a difference?' They were laughing as they left Maggie's yard by the back gate. Maggie rushed to bolt it, then turned to the outhouse.

'Jake,' she whispered. 'Jake, they've gone. It's safe.'

Suddenly, the pile of boxes came tumbling down and there, dusting himself down as he emerged from his hiding place, was Jake.

'Oh, Jake. I was so worried about you. The rat? Did you know they were scared of rats?'

'No, it was in the same corner that I wanted to be in, so I had to kill it. I just kicked it out of the way.' The nerves that Maggie had tried to keep under control while the soldiers had been there now began to take their toll.

'Why, Maggie, you're trembling!' Worried she might faint, Jake put his hands out to steady her. They stood in silence for a moment, Jake's hands around her waist. Jake sensed that there would never be another time so right.

This was the moment. He drew her towards him, and as their bodies touched, he felt something like electricity pass between them. Their eyes met, and then he lowered his head, and they kissed - a long, loving and tender kiss.

'Cooee!' Had two minutes passed, or was it five minutes? Jake had no idea. Reluctantly, Maggie pulled away.

'Mum's home.'

Later that day, Jake returned to the hotel room.

'How was it?' asked Sadie.

'What?' said Jake, blushing.

'The scooty-bob. You said you were going to test it.'

'Oh, it was excellent. No problems at all,' replied Jake, relieved.

'And did it cope with carrying the box of candles?'

'Oh dear, I forgot to get one.'

'Ecky thump! I thought that was the reason you were...oh, never mind.'

'Your ears have gone bright red, Jake,' commented Charlotte, 'Have you got a fever?'

'Fièvre d'amour,' whispered Genevieve.

Jake didn't answer and instead buried his nose in one of his notebooks, as though trying to study. Meanwhile, the three girls once again struggled to contain their laughter.

CHAPTER EIGHTEEN

'I'm really quite nervous,' said Genevieve. 'I've never been in an airship before.'

'There's no need to be bloomin' nervous, said Billy. 'Charlotte is a bleedin' brilliant pilot; I reckon she's better than Oliver.'

'Just look on it as a day's sightseeing. You are much safer up here than down there with all the strikers and protesters,' said Charlotte.

It was the day of the strike. It wasn't a national shutdown, though; employees of the Steam Works were at work as usual. Hastings and his men had ensured a full turnout the previous day by circulating among the workforce, armed with coshes, and making it clear just how much violence they would mete out to anyone who dared to join the strike. Just as Jake had predicted, those individuals would be deemed unfit for work and would be sacked. However, the authorities feared the worst, and every policeman and soldier was on duty.

The marching workers assembled in Trafalgar Square to listen to speeches from their leaders, most notably Jacky Storm. High above hovered the Rebel, piloted by Charlotte with Billy, Joshua and Genevieve aboard.

Oliver had disgraced himself once again. He should have been airborne as well but had arrived at the hotel the previous evening so drunk he could hardly stand.

'What is he wearing?' Sadie had gasped, for Oliver was dressed in a full set of women's clothes.

'Blimey! 'exclaimed Billy, 'I'm used to him leaving his hat or his gloves behind when he goes on a bender but not losing all his clobber!'

Not surprisingly, when the crew had tried to rouse him that morning, he was in no fit state to travel.

Edward was in the crowd below, taking notes for a report for Reuters, but he had already been helpful to the Rebels by dropping into the hotel the previous evening with a map of the route the marchers would take.

Now, as planned, with Joshua and Genevieve keeping their eyes on the ground below and Billy scanning the skies on the lookout for the Air-Fleet, Charlotte followed the route of the proposed march. The Trades Union had decided to march from Trafalgar Square along the Strand to Waterloo Bridge, then across to South London and through the working-class areas of Southwark and Lambeth before crossing back over the Thames via Westminster Bridge and on to the Houses of Parliament. After completing the route, Charlotte piloted the Rebel to St James' Park, where she knew Jake would be waiting near the lake.

Joshua lowered the rope and harness, and soon Jake was aboard the Rebel.

'Is Sadie safe?' asked Charlotte.

'Yes, she's having a cream tea in a little restaurant where they appear oblivious to the turmoil happening elsewhere in London. Have you anything to report?'

It's not good, I'm afraid. There are troops spread out all along the route, but we expected that. The problem will be when the protesters try to cross Westminster Bridge. The new machine you described, The Beast, is sitting on the bridge at the halfway point. It's difficult to imagine how they can get past it. In fact, I reckon it will be impossible and I hate to think about all the casualties if they try. On the other hand, the route from the other direction to the Houses of Parliament, along Whitehall, is relatively unguarded.

'I'll collect Sadie, then we'll get over to Trafalgar Square as quickly as we can and persuade them to come in through the back door,' said Jake. 'Don't forget about those adjustments to Rebel's controls I made.'

'Oh, Jake! You are always fiddling with it,' snapped Charlotte. 'Remind me what they do again.'

'It's that blue lever and the yellow one. The blue one will lock the steering to whatever you have set it to, both the direction and the altitude. The yellow one does the same, but it's on a timer. After thirty minutes, a warning bell will sound just before it deactivates itself. Be careful, though, because who knows what direction the Rebel will choose to fly with no one at the helm!

'I suppose the blue one will be useful, say, if I'm flying through the night above the clouds and I want to take a short break,' admitted Charlotte. 'Where's your boardy-skate, by the way?' Jake rolled his eyes and took a deep breath.

'My mono-scoot is hidden under a bush in the park.'

'Oh, this is fun,' yelled Sadie as they sped along The Mall on their way to Trafalgar Square. She was standing behind Jake, clinging onto him, her petticoats flying out behind her, showing an indecent amount of leg for the sensibilities of the day. 'I want one; make me one, please, Jake.' Jake smiled; he was enjoying the ride too. After the embarrassing episode in the hotel room, he had been rather wary of employing the steam boost, but on the straight run of The Mall, it caused no problem. Jake discovered that once he was travelling at speed, he could disengage the clockwork engine and freewheel. 'I must invent some kind of speed dial to tell me when to start the engine again,' he thought. 'Nearly there!' he called. They could hear the sound of the crowd cheering the speakers. He stopped the mono-scoot and they dismounted. Jake pointed. 'Wait over there behind the fountain with my mono-scoot, Sadie. I'll try and force my way through the crowd to get to the front.'

That was easier said than done; the protesters were jammed in tight. The speakers stood on a platform the organisers had erected at the foot of Nelson's Column. Jake noticed four enormous sculpted lions that hadn't been there the last time he visited the square, and standing on top of each, striking a heroic pose, was a protestor waving a Trades Union banner.

'Brothers!' Jacky Storm shouted, 'For too long, we have been under the boot of our oppressors, but today, my friends, is the day all that will change!' He paused to allow his supporters to cheer. 'Just like these noble lions here, we will open our mouths and roar and bite clean through the boots of those who seek to trample on us.' Jacky paused, confident in the knowledge that everyone was completely behind him, and strode around the platform, waving in acknowledgement of the crowd's support. Meanwhile, Jake had reached the foot of Nelson's Column. Until now, he had acted purely instinctively, but he was unsure of what to do in the face of such a charismatic speaker. He realised he needed to take advantage of the pause in the proceedings and stumbled onto the platform. It had not occurred to the organisers that anyone would attempt to join Jackie Storm on the stage, so no one barred Jake's way.

'Erm,' quavered Jake, overtaken by nerves.

'What have we here?' Jacky put his hands on his hips and looked Jake up and down. As the organisers started to try and apprehend Jake, Jacky, comfortable in his own ability to deal with the situation, waved them away.

'Erm, you, you mustn't cross Westminster Bridge; they are waiting for you,' stammered Jake.

'He says we mustn't cross the bridge because they are waiting for us,' shouted Jacky, then he started to laugh. 'Of course, they are waiting for us, and I'll tell you what! They'll be trembling with fear.'

'No, no! They have a new weapon.'

'A new weapon, he says. If you want to see a mighty weapon, look no further than the power of the working man!' The crowd roared in response.

Two people in the crowd knew Jake: Sadie, peeping out from behind the fountain and Edward, who was quite close to the front. They both realised that Jake was hopelessly out of his depth. For a start, he didn't look right. Jacky had purposely styled himself as a working man to suit his audience, so whilst he had many suits hanging in his wardrobe, today he sported a simple leather waistcoat and wore his white shirt without a tie and with the sleeves rolled up. In contrast, Jake's clothes looked completely out of place at this rally: The leather gloves he used to conceal his metal hand and avoid attracting attention; his top hat, decorated with cogs; his silk scarf, embroidered waistcoat and tailored jacket all contrived to give the impression that he was a boss, not a worker. Then, there was the fact that Jacky was a stocky, powerfully built man, the epitome of someone no stranger to hard graft, whereas Jake's slight and slender figure conveyed a completely different impression. How ironic, thought Edward; it was many, many years since Jacky had worked in industry, whereas until fairly recently, Jake had been a factory cleaner.

Put simply, although both men had clever minds, Jacky was an extravert and knew how to hold the attention of a crowd, whereas Jake, was an introvert, brilliant at thinking through a problem, applying logic and knowledge and then getting on with the task on his own. Jake had found himself in Jacky's domain and didn't know how to deal with it. Someone shouted up from the audience:

'I know who he is - he's one of them Rebel Runaways!' In an instant, Jacky seized on this; he had heard of them, although he had never read the stories.

'So what we have here, my friends, is a character from the Penny Dreadfuls,' he shouted, then turning towards Jake, he continued, still playing to his audience, 'So, my friend. Let me welcome you to the real world - the world of blood and sweat where real men toil to earn a crust, where the line between life and death is thinner than a hair from my head. And where we say enough is enough is enough.'

Edward and Sadie winced at the final indignity.

'We have no time for fancy hats. We are happy to let

the rain beat down on our bare heads and wash away the sorrows endured through lifetimes,' Jacky declared, and he grabbed Jake's top hat and flung it into the crowd. Then, with what looked like a friendly slap on the back but was really a powerful push, he propelled Jake off the stage. 'Come, my friend, join the working people, the salt of the earth!' The force of Jacky's shove caused Jake to stumble and fall head-first onto the ground below the platform, laughter ringing in his ears.

A woman helped him to his feet.

'Don't you worry pet. There's not many people get one over on Jacky Storm. I should know - he's my husband!' Just then, the bell from St Martin-in-the-Fields' church tolled the hour. It was time for the march to begin. Jake found himself struggling against the tide of marchers. Then, thankfully there was someone to help him; it was Edward.

'The fountain,' gasped Jake, 'I need to get to the fountain. Sadie's waiting there. Oh, that was terrible. Just terrible!'

As the Rebel began to climb after dropping Jake off in the park, Billy shouted in alarm.

'Cor blimey! There's another bleedin' airship behind us, and it's 'catchin' up bloomin' fast.' Charlotte immediately veered to the right and glanced through the starboard window to see an Air-Fleet craft approaching at speed. She pulled hard on the lever that would take the Rebel higher.

'Billy!' she shouted, 'Make sure the clockwork motor is fully wound up. We may need all the speed we can get.' As Billy turned the key, he saw that Charlotte showed no sign of panic. He had seen her like this before on the Rebel; she was completely calm and focused when there was a crisis.

'Alright,' she said, 'So you think you can fly an airship, do you? Let's see what you are made of!' They were up high now; below, she could see the blue line of the Thames, snaking through London, and she put the Rebel into a steep dive, heading straight for the river.

Wing Commander Curbishly was at the helm of the airship chasing the Rebel. It had got the better of him once before, and he was determined that it wouldn't happen again. Despite Oliver's low opinion of his intelligence, Curbishly was a good pilot.

'Don't think you can get away from me that easily,' he muttered, then shouted to his crew, 'I'm going to get close in behind so we will get dragged along in their slipstream.' He adjusted his controls to follow Charlotte's descent.

Billy bit his lip. He wanted to cry out because, to him, it looked like they were in a suicide dive. However, he had complete faith in Charlotte, and he wanted to appear brave in front of Genevieve, so he gripped the edge of his seat so hard that his knuckles turned white. Joshua, on the other hand, was making whooping noises; he found it thrilling. Genevieve failed to see, because her eyes were tightly closed, that at the last minute, Charlotte levelled out the Rebel, so she skimmed along a few inches above the water. Although Curbishley knew the airship he was following would have to change direction eventually, he was a little taken aback by how late she left it. On this occasion, his steering was not as adept as Charlotte's. The rear of his gondola slammed against the water, causing a window to shatter before he could steady his airship once again to fall in line behind the Rebel.

'Ee, Jake lad!' said Sadie, 'Don't take it so hard. You were in an impossible situation. Nothing was going to change Jacky Storm's mind. He would have looked weak if he had backed down, and with men like that, no matter which side of the fence they are on politically, power is everything.'

'But I was so feeble,' wailed Jake.

'Not everyone can be good at everything,' said Edward, 'You have a brilliant mind. You can harness your interest in science and engineering to make fabulous inventions. Where does it say that you must be good at public speaking too?'

'From a blank sheet of paper, you can conjure up a wonderful machine. Out of nowhere, you can snap your fingers and come up with a plan. That's what we need now. We need you!' implored Sadie. Jake was silent for a moment, then he straightened up. It was almost as though he had grown two inches. With a glint in his eye; the old Jake was back.

'I need to get behind the lines, to the Westminster side of the bridge,' he said.

'Ah! That might be difficult. There will be a lot of security checks,' replied Edward. Jake's face fell, 'But don't worry; I've already got permission to be there, in my capacity as a Reuters reporter. You can use my pass.' Edward drew a folded piece of paper from his jacket pocket. 'However, you may have to sign something to gain entrance, so you should practise my signature.' Jake studied the pass for a few moments.

'That's alright, I've got it.' Edward smiled; he had forgotten about Jake's remarkable ability to memorise. Jake placed the document in a leather satchel that was hooked on the back of his mono-scoot. 'I'm ready for action!'

'Sadie and I will catch up with the marchers and follow events from their perspective. We will see you later,' said Edward. Sadie gave Jake a peck on the cheek:

'Good luck, Jake, we have faith in you!'

It was Mary Smethers' first day working in the Births, Marriages and Deaths Registration Department at Somerset House. The morning had been somewhat tedious, and she was worried that she was facing a lifetime of monotony in which nothing exciting ever happened. The only saving grace was that her desk was close to the window, so when her supervisor wasn't watching, she would sneak a look at the busy River Thames. Out of the corner of her eye, she saw two dark shapes pass the window. Risking admonishment, she rushed to get a better view.

'Goodness!' she exclaimed, 'Just look at this!' Mary's colleagues clustered around the window and watched in amazement as two low-flying airships zig-zagged along the river.

Charlotte swung hard on the helm of the Rebel.

'Let's see how you like this!' She trained her sights on the grand building overlooking the river and continued at full speed, the Air-Fleet ship following in her wake. As she was leading the chase, she had a good view of the building and as she approached could even pick out an audience lining the windows. She timed her action beautifully; at the last minute, she swung the Rebel around in a U-turn. Curbishley tried to copy her, but the few extra seconds it took him to realise what was happening were vital.

Mary had screamed when she saw the first airship

heading straight towards her, thankfully changing direction just in time, but when the nose of the second airship bounced off the building, pushing the window frame into the room and showering her with broken glass, she screamed even louder and continued to scream for a full five minutes. So great was the shock that it was to be the last day in all her working life that she wished for something exciting to happen.

'Oh dear!' said Charlotte, looking behind at the pursuing airship. 'You've scraped all your paintwork. You are not looking so fine and dandy now!'

'Now then. What's your name?' asked a soldier seated behind a trestle table.

'Edward Ramsey,' replied Jake. The soldier ran his finger down a long list of names with agonising slowness:

'There. Gotcha! Let me inspect your pass. Now, sign here and here...and here.' The soldier compared the signatures for longer than Jake thought necessary. Then he noticed Jake's mono-scoot. 'What's that?'

'It's a mobile tele-sender,' said Jake confidently.

'What's that when it's at home?'

'Well, as you know from my security pass, I'm a reporter for Reuters. We are the first news organisation to make use of the telegraph service to send our reports far and wide. This is a mobile device which enables me to send messages back to the office. I tap out my new stories using that button, in Morse code.'

'Really? Do you know Morse Code? What's my name in Morse then?'

'What is your name?

'It's Pip.' This was all taking longer than Jake had

hoped, so thank goodness it was a short name. Jake tapped it out on the table:

'That's easy. It's dot, dash, dash, dot, that's "P", then dot, dot for "I", and then dot, dash, dash, dot again.'

'Hurry up!' Others waiting in the queue were getting impatient. The soldier handed the pass back to Jake, who hurriedly pushed his mono-scoot towards Westminster Bridge.

'Oh no!' Jake realised that not only were the protesters already on the bridge, but also there were dozens and dozens of soldiers between him and Fotheringay's crowd-control machine, the Beast. For the moment, there appeared to be a standoff. The front line of soldiers was poised, their muskets trained on the protesters. On the bridge, waving a banner and with his back to the army, the unmistakable figure of Jacky Storm was rallying his supporters. Jake pushed along the crowded bridge shouting, 'Reporter coming through!' With a growing sense of doom, he watched the situation escalate. Jacky turned, raised his banner and started to run towards the soldiers like a warrior king leading a battle charge. Whether Jacky would have remained at the front or slowed to allow himself to be enveloped by the others, Jake would never know. The soldiers operating the crowd-control machine were ready for this moment. First, a burst of ballbearings showered the marchers. The red spots that bloomed on Jacky's shirt didn't stop him; they merely enraged him. Jake was still fighting to get closer and realised that the soldiers were waiting for Jacky to come within range. Then to his horror, Jake saw a cannon emit a piercing jet of high-pressured steam, which arced towards Jacky, stopping him in his tracks. Jacky screamed, and for a moment, Jake saw the scalded face of the Trades Union man erupt into boils, before he slumped to the ground. Next, soldiers in the front line fired their muskets and several protesters also fell. A jet of water from the third cannon sprayed over the stunned crowd. A few brave individuals fought through the torrent of water, grabbed Jacky Storm, and dragged him back into the midst of the protesters. It looked very much as though the authorities had defeated the workers.

By now, Jake had reached the waggon. What he needed was a diversion, and then, as if in answer to his prayers, Charlotte obliged. To everyone's amazement the Rebel came swooping in just a few feet above the surface of the Thames, aiming straight for them and followed by an Air-Fleet airship. Then everyone ducked as the two ships roared over the bridge with just inches to spare. This was the moment for Jake to take action!

CHAPTER NINETEEN

'So, he thinks he can outmanoeuvre me, does he?' sneered Curbishly to his crew, 'Well, he's got another think coming!' It would never have occurred to Curbishly in a million years that a woman was piloting the Rebel! He assumed it was Oliver. The crew were a little perturbed that, in the last pass over a bridge, the gondola had scraped against the ornamental railings, and now they could see daylight through the decking.

Despite the danger, Charlotte was enjoying herself. The chase allowed her to test her flying skills and put the Rebel through its paces. She could tell by looking over her shoulder at Billy and Genevieve, who were both spending much of their time with their eyes screwed shut, that flying like this would never be the norm. She made the Rebel shoot up into the air and then spun the tail around, to go back down the river the way they had come. She gave a wide birth to passing cargo ships on their way to and from the dockside warehouses in the Pool of London. She didn't want to risk the lives of the seamen by causing her pursuer crash into them.

'Ha! Look! Tower Bridge is open.' The two levered sections, the bascules, had been raised to allow a sailing ship to pass through. Charlotte dropped to just above the water and skimmed through the opening. It wasn't until then that she realised the bascules had started to close, something that Curbishly would soon discover!

'Ha ha! Look!' laughed Billy, who was jumping up and down in excitement. 'They're only bleedin' trapped under the bloomin' bridge!' Charlotte circled for a better view and saw that a quick-witted operator had raised the bascules, lifting the Air-Fleet high above the river. Joshua laughed at the sight of water pouring from its gondola.

'They must have been flooded in there.'

'So, you've had a taste of low-level flying. Let's see how you deal with height!' cried Charlotte.

When Charlotte flew over the bridge, all eyes were on the Rebel. Jake took advantage of the distraction to kick away the nearest wooden chock wedged against the front wheel of the Tiberius waggon. He darted around to the far side and dispensed with the other brake as well. The waggon didn't move as it was on a flat part of the bridge. No one noticed him; the guards were all transfixed by the spectacle of the two giant aircraft snaking up and down the river almost like a circus act. The next part of Jake's plan was the easiest. If anyone observed him, Jake would seem to be affectionately patting the two giant gas canisters on the back of the waggon as if to say, 'Well done, Beast!' What he was actually doing, however, was placing two magnetic clockwork spiders on them. He had redesigned these to cut a small hole through metal, and just like the one he had employed on the Deception, they immediately stretched out their legs and started to spin round.

While the spiders did their work, Jake looked to see what was happening at the other end of the bridge. The protesters, too, had been momentarily distracted by the airships. Now, confusion spread through their ranks: on the one hand they were leaderless and unable to stomach facing such lethal firepower; on the other hand, they were unwilling to retreat, for then all their sacrifices would have been for nothing.

A shrill whistle split the air, increasing in volume as another joined it. The spiders had completed their mission. Unlike on the Deception, when the spiders dropped through the holes they had created, this time they met a high-powered jet of stream which propelled them far away, too fast for Jake to see where they went. At first, Jake was disappointed that nothing else happened. He leant on the waggon, which was enough to start the momentum. Slowly at first but quickly gathering speed, the waggon started to trundle down the bridge heading straight for the protesters, powered by two jets of steam. Seeing themselves being delivered to the strikers, the three soldiers who had been operating the cannons leapt off the waggon, which was now travelling at an alarming speed. At first, there was consternation amongst the protesters at the sight of the Beast heading towards them. However, when they parted to let it pass by, an enormous cheer rose as they realised it was driverless. Eventually, the waggon crashed into the railings, whereupon the protesters duly helped it on its way, and through sheer manpower and brute strength, fuelled by the horrors of what they had seen that day, they toppled the Beast into the Thames. Steam screamed from the canisters until, eventually, in a cascade of bubbles, the Beast disappeared below the surface. Then, fired up by this triumph, the protesters charged at their aggressors. Distracted by the airships, many soldiers hadn't reloaded their muskets, and they turned and ran. Others managed to fire a shot, but then realising they had no time to reload, they too fled. Soon the bridge was completely in the hands of the workers, and there was nothing to stop them from marching on to Westminster.

'Open sky, here we come!' cried Charlotte, and she set the controls for a steady climb at top speed. Billy sighed in relief. He had found the riverside manoeuvres far from enjoyable.

'Where do they think they are going?' scoffed Curbishly. 'There's no hiding place up there.'

Charlotte looked behind her and noticed several of the gondola's windows were open. Billy had unfastened them in case he needed to be sick.

'Let's get the Rebel closed up,' she called, 'The higher we go, the thinner the air will be. We may as well keep the air we've got for as long as possible. I'll help.' Charlotte looked at the two new levers that Jake had installed so that the Rebel would fly itself. She pondered which one to use, then selected the yellow one: the lever incorporating a clockwork timer.

All the windows had catches that could be tightened by turning a knob, and while the airship flew onwards and upwards, the crew busied themselves shutting them all.

'The other airship ain't got this option,' said Billy, "Cause I noticed half of their bleedin' windows is bashed out! He ain't such a good pilot as you, Charlotte!'

'I think I'll have to sit down for a while and rest,' said Joshua once the windows were all tightly closed.

'I ain't surprised,' replied Billy. You've been dancing around the whole time we've been flying.'

'I've always loved the thrill of the hunt,' laughed Joshua, 'Only it makes a change to be the prey!'

'Well, this is a novelty!' remarked Charlotte. 'Being in charge of the Rebel but sitting at the back in comfort.'

'It's tiring, all this being chased about business,' said Billy. 'I'm feeling sleepy.'

'I suppose I had better get back to the helm,' said Charlotte, standing up, 'Goodness! I feel a bit dizzy,' and she promptly sat down again.

'Ohhh!' moaned Joshua, 'I have a terrible headache.'

'Give me a few moments and I'll get back to the home. No, not home; I'll get back to the wheel thing. What's it called again? Helm. That's it, helm. It's all so confusing. I'll just close my eyes for a moment and wait for my head to clear.'

The Air-Fleet airship was now far behind them, flying in a somewhat erratic fashion, but the Rebel sailed on, steadily gaining height whilst, inside the gondola, all four crew members were slumped unconscious in their seats.

Sadie and Edward were following behind the marchers. As they neared Westminster Bridge, they saw a stream of casualties moving towards them. Some were walking wounded, some were supported by fellow protesters and others were bloodied and lifeless.

'Oh dear!' sighed Sadie. 'It looks like it hasn't been going very well.'

'I recognise that woman,' said Edward. 'I saw her at the meeting, and she was the one who helped Jake to his feet after he was pushed into the crowd. I'm pretty sure she's Jacky Storm's wife.' Sadie looked over to see a stony-faced woman following a handcart pulled by two men. Stretched out on the cart was the body of a man, covered by several Trades Union banners.

'Excuse me,' asked Edward, 'Is that, is that...'

'Aye, it's my Jacky,' she said, 'He's gone to meet his maker.'

'Oh, I am sorry,' replied Edward. 'He was a good man who stood by his principles. I'm a reporter. How did it happen?'

'He was at the front of the march and they were waiting for him with that giant cannon machine. He should have listened to that young man on the platform.'

'That was my friend, Jake,' said Sadie, 'We are two of the Rebel Runaways.'

'Thank God something went wrong with the cannon. It just set off into our marchers on its own, and now it's at the bottom of the Thames.'

'That will have been Jake's doing too. I just know it. He left us to go and sabotage it.'

'I'll make sure everyone knows that our Jacky was wrong about you lot. He was no saint and God knows he could be too stubborn for his own good.'

'I'll make sure I write an honest account of what happened,' said Edward. 'The national press are all in the pocket of this new Government. You won't find the truth on their pages.'

'We had better go and find Jake,' said Sadie, 'Goodbye, Mrs Storm. Our condolences to you.'

Jake was unsure what to do next. He scanned the skies, but there was no sign of the Rebel. He didn't know if that was a good thing or a bad thing. He decided the best way to meet up with Edward and Sadie would be to wait on the bridge, as they would have to pass that way eventually, whereas if he followed the marchers to the Houses of Parliament, he would surely lose them in the crowd. After his experiences earlier in the day, Jake had had enough of listening to political speeches.

'I know!' he thought. 'I'll go and look for my spiders. They will have rolled up into a ball.' Jake worked his way back along the bridge, starting from where the waggon had been positioned, his eyes fixed on the ground. Either he would find the spiders, or Edward and Sadie would find him first. In the event someone else found him, someone altogether more disagreeable!

'Wake up, wake up! Charlotte, wake up!' implored Genevieve, dabbing Charlotte's face with a wet cloth.

'Where am I? moaned Charlotte, opening her eyes.

'You're in the Rebel, and we are spinning round and round, and I don't know what to do.'

Suddenly it all came flooding back. The airship had been climbing using the automatic timer setting, but it must have cancelled itself after thirty minutes. Jake had warned her that he didn't know what the Rebel would do if left unattended. Charlotte rushed over to the helm; she still felt dizzy because the atmosphere was thin, but at least they were no longer climbing. Taking control of the airship once more, she took her down.

'Genevieve, please tend to Billy and Joshua; try to rouse them and open a few windows. We need a change of air.' Eventually, Joshua and Billy spluttered back to consciousness, helped by a generous dose of water splashed in their faces!

'Bleedin' 'ell, I fought my cakes was burnin',' complained Billy.

'Ohhh!' groaned Joshua, 'I was fighting a demon!'

'Did you win?' asked Billy.

'I'm here, aren't I? laughed Joshua.

As the fog in Charlotte's head cleared, she suddenly remembered what had caused them to get into this predicament.

'Any sign of the Air-Fleet?'

'They're not behind us,' said Joshua.

'Wait! 'Ave a butchers down there. Ain't that them?' yelled Billy. Far below them, they could see the battered airship drifting aimlessly, first travelling sideways, then being blown backwards.

'It looks to me like no one is at the helm,' mused Charlotte. 'The Rebel was probably behaving in a similar fashion when we were out cold.'

'Cor blimey, I declare us the winners! Hoorah!' sang out Billy. 'Ain't we going back now?'

'I suppose we ought to, but doesn't their airship look sad? Like a wounded animal.'

'But they were chasing us!' said Billy, 'They deserve it.'

'It's not so much the crew I feel sorry for, although they would have been just obeying orders. No, it's the airship. It doesn't seem right, leaving it to die.'

'What do you want us to do?' asked Joshua. Charlotte

thought for a moment:

'If I hover over it, do you mind getting in the harness and going down to look through the windows?'

Five minutes later, if any of the crew had been awake, they would have been astonished to see an upside-down face peering into the gondola. Joshua could make out five crew members slumped on the floor, and the pilot collapsed at the helm. Charlotte and Joshua had formed a plan, and it quite literally swung into action as Joshua went flying through the window. He secured his harness to the door and left the heavier of the two ropes that he had brought with him there. Then he dragged the pilot over to join the other crew members and quickly tied them all together. He and Charlotte had decided it would be safer to do that first and then see if they were alive. Joshua nodded, they were all alive, but now there was no chance of them overpowering him. The next part of the plan was trial and error. Joshua had to attempt to turn off the engine. Charlotte had given him a few clues as to what he might try, but she only had experience of the Rebel's controls, so she couldn't be positive about how to shut down the Air-Fleet ship. Eventually, Joshua was satisfied that none of the propellers appeared to be turning. One of the crew members was coming to, and Joshua flashed him a smile before donning his harness, grabbing the spare coil of rope and leaping out of the window. Once Charlotte saw him emerge, she edged the Rebel forwards until Joshua was dangling directly over the nose of the Air-Fleet ship. He sat astride it for a few moments, revelling in the feeling that he was riding a wild bull, before tying one end of the rope to the docking ring and swinging free to be winched back up to the Rebel. Before climbing in, he made fast the other end of the rope just below the doorway.

'Well done, Joshua. Excellent work,' smiled Charlotte, 'Now we can tow her back into the City, and I know just the place to tie her up. The last time we passed Westminster it looked like the strikers had made it through to the Houses of Parliament, so they will get a good view of the Air-Fleet ship if we tie her to Big Ben. Mind you, we'll have to be quick; they will have to send up a balloon or another airship to investigate, and we had better not be around when they arrive or they'll give chase.'

'Oh no!' groaned Billy, 'I can't face all that malarkey again!'

Jake had found one of the spiders nestled against the bridge railings, and he realised there was a chance the other one had rolled right through them into the river and been lost. Nevertheless, he didn't give up searching. He continued to zig-zag along the bridge, oblivious to the last of the marchers streaming across, until he was stopped in his tracks by feeling something hard pressing against his temple.

'I know what that is,' he thought with dread.

'At last. It's you, Hooky. You may think yourself a fancy la-di-da, but you'll always be Hooky to me!'

Jake not only knew what it was now - it was a pistol - but also who it was. He was in dire straits because he was at close quarters with none other than his arch-enemy, Hastings!

Oliver had told the crew not to be unduly worried when faced with someone aiming a pistol at them. The weapons were so wildly inaccurate that they would be extremely unlucky to get in the way of a bullet. However, in this case, Jake realised that Hastings could hardly miss at this distance, so death would be inevitable. If Jake had had his dart-firing hand fitted, it might have been a different matter, but wanting to look as normal as possible, he was wearing his regular hand, albeit concealed by a leather glove.

'Don't think I'm going to risk losing you by attempting to hand you in. You are going to end your days right here on this bridge. Look at me! I want to see the fear in your eyes.'

Slowly, Jake raised his head to look his nemesis directly in the eye. Hastings was going to be disappointed because what Jake felt in his heart was loathing for this bully of a man and all he stood for. He hoped that these thoughts would transmit through his eyes. What those eyes did see, was a flash of steel, followed by the sound of the pistol firing and then someone roaring in pain. Jake was amazed to find he was still alive!

'My deepest apologies for being late to the party,' said Oliver, hooking his sword stick under Hastings' pistol, which a blow from that weapon had forced him to drop. With a deft flick of Oliver's wrist it went spinning through the air and into the river. The yelling was coming from Hastings, who was sitting on the ground, trying to remove his boot and gazing in disbelief at the wound he had inflicted on himself when he had involuntarily pulled the trigger. The end of his boot was missing, and also, no doubt, was his big toe. 'I heard that you lost a finger during that testing a little while ago, and now this!' said Oliver with feigned concern. 'My dear chap, you simply must look after your extremities. Still, we won't keep you. We have to go and join the party.' Oliver patted Jake on the back, and they turned and started to walk away. Jake paused.

'That was awfully good timing, Oliver.'

'Happy to oblige, dear chap.'

'Actually, I was on the bridge because I hoped to see Sadie and Edward pass this way.'

Oliver and Jake did not know that, not only did Hastings possess a second pistol, but that also, in his anger and pain, he was training it on their backs. Inaccurate or not, there was a good chance he would hit one of them as they hadn't walked far. Oliver and Jake were alerted to this tricky situation by hearing another scream from Hastings. They turned to see him clutching his arm where a dart protruded from his bicep.

'I must be losin' me touch,' frowned Sadie as she and Edward joined Jake and Oliver, 'I was aiming for his heart!'

CHAPTER TWENTY

'Pass me some o' that bacon, please,' said Billy, 'It's cooked just the way I like it.'

'I'll send your compliments to the chef,' laughed Oliver, 'I'm sure you will make Mario's day!'

'Thanks for booking the restaurant for this private breakfast for us all, Oliver,' said Charlotte.

'It's been very useful to hear all the different versions of yesterday's events,' said Edward, 'I have so much material for the Chronicles that I will have to start writing serials.'

'It was terrifying,' said Genevieve. 'I'm not sure I'm up to all this excitement.'

'Don't you worry. We can't all be swashbucklers. You'll come into your own when we start the Fashion

House,' reassured Charlotte.

'Old Mario 'ad a bleedin' good giggle when he heard what had happened to Hastings,' chuckled Billy.

'Especially when he found out that he was the same man who had knocked over one of his waiters when he was chasing you, Billy,' said Sadie.

'Mario told me,' said Billy, 'That he 'ad threatened to chop off Hastings...'

'Let's not continue with this subject,' interrupted Charlotte, 'I'm still eating! Anyway, we shouldn't laugh at his misfortune.' She tried to keep a straight face,but lasted only a few seconds before dissolving into laughter, joined by the others.

'It's a good job you tethered the Air-Fleet craft up high,' said Edward.

'Why?' asked Charlotte.

'As you know, the strikers lit a lot of bonfires and were sitting around them singing songs late into the night. After you all left, the youthful element in the crowd was having a competition to try and hit the airship with burning branches from the fire. They didn't get anywhere close, as you can imagine, but just think what would have happened if you had left the airship within range.'

'It doesn't bear thinking about,' said Oliver, 'I'm sure they didn't realise just how explosive hydrogen is. It could have turned Big Ben into very small Ben!'

'Actually,' said Jake, 'I've been reading about a gas called helium. Have you heard of it?' Everyone shook their head. 'It will make an excellent substitute for hydrogen. It's lighter than air, and it's non-flammable.'

'Excellent! Let's switch to helium. Where do we get it?' asked Oliver.

'Erm, Texas.'

'Then that's where we shall go!'

Where the bleedin' 'ell is Texas?' asked Billy.

'It's in America.'

'Stone the crows! We can't go there until we see Lady Whatchamacallit and get me soup stations set up.'

'And we can't go until we've been to Paris and we've set up our Fashion House,' added Sadie.

'We have to go to Bristol, too - I need some more parts,' said Jake.

'Is that to make me a scooty-skate?' asked Sadie excitedly.

'A mono-scoot. Yes, it is.'

'Please, can I have one that fires darts?'

'It looks like we have many adventures ahead,' said Oliver, 'I don't know when I'll get any rest!'

'Says the man who was snoring away when we went to join the march yesterday,' remarked Sadie.

'Ah, yes,' replied Oliver, 'It's time I turned over a new leaf; let's make a toast to new beginnings; Mario will have a bottle of...'

'Oliver! It's breakfast time! You should be satisfied with a cup of tea!'

'Hmm,' replied Oliver in a voice that indicated he was far from convinced. 'First stop will be Manhattan. I had a drink once called a Manhattan. Now there's something I look forward to trying again! And Texas; should be able to buy Tequila there. I've never tried it, but I'm all for adventure. And of course, it's not far from there to Tennessee, well in airship miles that is. I'll buy you all a Tennessee whiskey, and...'

'Mario!' Charlotte's voice sang out, 'More tea, please!'

The End

A NOTE FROM THE AUTHOR

I hope you have enjoyed my book and will look out for other titles in the 'Rebel Runaways' series.

I want to thank Rachel Laurence for her input into all my books. As an actress, she does fantastic work narrating the audiobooks, but before that, she plays a crucial part in the editing process.

I am also the author of the 'Stuck' series from Amazon. They are stand-alone time travel books suitable for adults and children 8+. You can see them by visiting this page on my website: www.stuckdave.co.uk/blink

You can also join my mailing list and find information about upcoming publications and have the opportunity to win free stuff! I would love it if you followed me on Instagram, too: @stuckdavewrites

I would be extremely grateful if you could write a review of my book on Amazon. Even if you didn't buy this book yourself from Amazon, you could still post a review there.

The third book in the series, "Escape to the Skies" will be published in 2024

Escape to the Skies

The Rebel Runaways visit America and find the country divided by a Civil War. It's not their fight, but they can't help getting drawn into the conflict.

The Rebel Runaways have their sights set on revenge against a heartless spy, but he's a tricky customer and evades them in New York. Can they follow him south? They traverse the country in the airship, finding action and adventure are never far behind, but the Rebel Runaways find it's not just a simple case of picking sides.

Will they make the right choices? Can they survive?

www.ingramcontent.com/pod-product-compliance
Lightning Source LLC
Chambersburg PA
CBHW021709190726
48289CB00008B/2440